The Ghost Squad
Breaks Through

By the Same Author

The Ghost Squad Breaks Through

by E. W. Hildick

A Ghost Squad Book

E. P. DUTTON   NEW YORK

To the Skibbereen Angel
and all the other
friendly ghosts

LIBRARY OF CONGRESS CATALOGING IN PUBLICATION DATA

Hildick, E. W. (Edmund Wallace),
   The Ghost Squad breaks through.

   Summary: When one of them finds a successful way to
communicate with a live person, four young ghosts decide
to band together to help solve and prevent crimes.
   [1. Ghosts—Fiction.
2. Mystery and detective stories]   I. Title.
PZ7.H5463Gh   1984   [Fic]   84-3985
ISBN 0-525-44097-6

Published in the United States by E. P. Dutton, Inc.,
2 Park Avenue, New York, N.Y. 10016

Published simultaneously in Canada by
Fitzhenry & Whiteside Limited, Toronto

Editor: Julie Amper   Designer: Claire Counihan

Printed in the U.S.A.   COBE   First Edition
10 9 8 7 6 5 4 3 2 1

Contents

1
The Silent Witness

Danny Green was worried. There was an anxious frown on his pale thin face as he stood waiting at the edge of the railroad station parking lot. The frown made him look much older than most fourteen-year-olds. Really haggard.

And that wasn't the only strange thing about him.

Even stranger was the way that he was dressed. Across the street, outside the bank, the electronic clock/thermometer was changing from eighty-seven to eighty-eight degrees. Yet Danny was wearing a thick black imitation-leather windbreaker. All zippered up. With the collar up. And with a red nylon scarf!

The heat didn't seem to bother him at all. He was

much more interested in the time. When he saw it change to 4:14, his frown deepened.

"Come on! Come on!" he growled, looking up and down the street. "You shoulda been back more than an *hour* ago!"

The parking lot was just a rough cindered strip of land at the side of the tracks, unfenced. Only a few yards away from Danny, people were passing by on the sidewalk. He didn't bother keeping his voice down, yet nobody gave him a glance. Men, women and children dressed in light summer clothes, their faces deeply tanned, walked past—some of them sweating, some fanning themselves with newspapers. But even when they glanced across in his direction, nobody said: "Hey! Look at this freak, all bundled up!" Or: "How pale the poor boy looks! He must just have come out of the hospital!"

Danny might not have existed for all the interest anyone was showing. Even the two guys who came strolling up to the car next to him—one of them just missing treading on his toes—even they didn't take any notice. Not even when he groaned out loud: "Come on! Where *are* you?"

Not that Danny took much notice of them, either. At first.

In fact, he only seemed to become aware of their presence when one of them opened up the trunk of the car, an old black Plymouth, took a couple of Cokes out of a Styrofoam container, and said: "So that's it! That's the big, big jewelry store we're gonna hit on our first real job together! Beautiful!"

2

The speaker was about nineteen, slightly built, with short fair hair. His hard blue eyes darted angrily this way and that.

"Cut the sarcasm, Roscoe!" said the other. He was taller, heavier, with a dark beard. They were both dressed lightly in fawn slacks and white T-shirts, yet the bearded one seemed to be feeling the heat more. "I never said it was a big *store*. Just one big *pushover*. Which it is."

He slurped his Coke thoughtfully, staring across at the Hymans' place, three doors away from the bank on one side and two from the pool hall on the other.

"A dump!" said Roscoe.

"Maybe—but good for a couple of grands' worth of gold chains, rings, bracelets, come Friday night."

"Why Friday? Why not tonight?"

"Because Friday's the night Pop Hyman and his wife are guests of honor at the Vets' dinner, over in Sharonville. So there'll be nothing and nobody to come between us and the goodies save one Mickey Mouse alarm system. Which I can take out in five seconds flat."

They were speaking in low voices, but not so low that they didn't carry easily to Danny Green, less than three feet away. Danny's frown was different now. Not so much anxious as concerned. Mr. and Mrs. Hyman had been pretty good to him and his kid brothers and sisters.

"Yeah?" said Roscoe, crushing his empty can and giving the other guy an ugly grin. "And if I bring

3

along my piece, I can take out *Mom and Pop Hyman* in five seconds flat. So why wait till Friday?"

"Hey!" The bearded one looked alarmed. "Hey, cut that out! I thought we had a deal—no guns!"

Roscoe laughed and punched his friend's arm.

"Sure, Kelly! Sure! I was only kidding. This is your job, so you call the—uh—shots. So it's no guns." His eyes narrowed viciously. *"This* time."

"Any time!"

"Maybe. . . . Anyway, Friday it is. But you *sure* they'll be out at this dinner?"

"Positive. Listen. . . ."

As Kelly leaned into the trunk for another couple of cans, his voice became muffled and indistinct.

But Danny was no longer listening anyway. Out of the corner of his eye he'd seen the two kids he'd been waiting for so anxiously. They were dawdling along the sidewalk, headed toward him, their arms loaded with packages and their mouths full of candy.

His brother Mike was ten and his sister Jilly was eight. They were both thin and undersized. Danny stepped forward. They slowed down and stopped at the edge of the parking lot. But this wasn't because they were paying any attention to Danny.

"You tried this chocolate fudge, Mike? 's good!"

Jilly's voice was blurred with chocolate. There were smears of it all around her mouth. She held out one of the candies to Mike. He shook his head. Danny didn't blame him. The candy was melting in her fingers already.

4

But Mike was more interested in his own. He'd plugged his mouth with something that looked like licorice. A trickle of black juice was running down his chin.

Danny sighed. They were *always* buying candy these days. Right after school, they'd make it their very first job. Buying candy for themselves and the two younger ones. That was no way to look after themselves! They—

"Hey, *you!*"

Danny turned.

An older boy was coming toward them. There was nothing undersized about *him*. Chester Adams was fourteen, but he was already a good three inches taller than Danny, and beefy, too. His fat cheeks glowed with health. His piggy little eyes glittered with meanness.

Danny knew that look. So did Mike and Jilly. They bunched closer. They looked up at the newcomer, half-scared, half-defiant.

"I've been watching you guys!" said Chester.

He was stooping over Mike and Jilly. He stuck out a fat finger at the packages in Mike's hands.

"Look at you! . . . You, too!" The finger stabbed at Jilly's packages, making her shrink back. The piece of fudge in her fingers slid off and fell to the ground. On its way it glanced off Chester's right foot, smearing his white sneaker.

"Oh—sorry!" she said.

"You will be! Before I'm through. . . ." Chester

turned to Mike. "Like I said, I've been watching you guys. And every day I see you with your arms loaded with candy. Expensive stuff, some of it, too. I figure you must be spending more than ten dollars a day. Where're you getting the money?"

"Mom gives it to us," said Jilly, in a half-whisper.

"You're lying!"

"She"—Mike managed to get his wad of licorice out of the way of his tongue—"she *isn't* lying! It's true."

"I think you steal it."

"We *don't!*" said Jilly, beginning to look mad. "Mom—it—it's Mom's money!"

"Yeah! So you steal it from her purse. Or her house-keeping stash. But that's OK." Chester had dropped his voice. His eyes were still glittering, but an oily smile had appeared below them. "I'm not going to fink on you. So long as you give me a cut of whatever you get. Say fifty-fifty. Huh?"

"You get lost!"

Mike's eyes were like Danny's. A weak pale blue, and slightly popping. But now they were flashing, and Danny felt a surge of pride.

"Good kid!" he murmured.

But this was drowned by Chester's next words.

"Listen, *you!*" he growled, grabbing Mike by his shirt collar and twisting it so hard that the kid gave a strangled yelp and dropped a packet of sour balls. "Don't—you—ever—talk to me—like that—again!"

With every word or two, he gave the younger boy a savage shake. None of the passersby tried to stop this. Just another bunch of squabbling kids, their faces seemed to say. Danny was furious, though. So was Jilly. Tears of rage were trickling down her cheeks to join the chocolate.

But the difference between Jilly's fury and Danny's was that hers drove the little girl to do something about it.

Still clutching her packages, she swung back her right foot and kicked Chester on the shin. Good and hard.

"Hey!" he howled, releasing Mike and making a dash at Jilly. "You'll pay for that!"

Jilly darted past him, making for the crossing a few yards farther along. Mike panicked and veered over into the parking lot, heading for the space between the two nearest cars.

Chester had him before he'd made three strides.

"Gotcha!" he snarled, grabbing the kid—this time by the hair.

"Leave him be!" yelled Jilly, running back.

"You shove off!" growled Chester, sending her sprawling on the cinders.

And Danny?

What was *he* doing to help his kid brother and sister?

Nothing!

Nothing but *stand* there feeling sick to his stomach.

After all, what *could* he do?

Danny Green was a ghost!

2
"What Can Ghosts Do?"

Danny Green had been a ghost for more than four months. In that time, he'd learned a lot about what ghosts could and couldn't do.

Especially what they couldn't do.

First, they couldn't scare living people. Not all that easily.

If we could—oh boy!—wouldn't I throw a scare into that creep right now! he thought.

The bully was spelling out to Mike and Jilly what hard times he had in store for them if they didn't go along with his proposition. He still held Mike by the hair.

I mean, how can I scare him if I can't even make him *see* me? thought Danny, shoving his head in front of Chester's eyes—putting it slap between the bully and his brother—and making a horrible face.

Chester Adams didn't even blink.

And how can I scare him if I can't even make him *hear* me? Danny thought, putting his mouth close to Chester's right ear and hollering: "HEY! JERK!"

Chester Adams didn't even turn his head. He just went on saying ugly things to Mike and Jilly in a soft but nasty voice.

Or *feel* me? thought Danny, suddenly getting mad.

He grabbed Chester's ear and tried to give it a fierce twist.

But all Chester did was absentmindedly give that ear a flick like he'd felt a fly brush against it.

Joe Armstrong had told Danny about that. Joe was an older ghost, and in the eighteen months he'd been haunting the town he'd run tests on living people—touching them and observing their reactions.

"All they feel is a slight coolness, Danny. No matter how hard you hit them or squeeze them or pull them, all they get is a very faint shiver. Sometimes they don't even notice it. And when they do they usually joke about it."

"Joke?"

"Yeah. I bet you did it yourself when you were alive. I bet when you felt an unexplained shiver, you said: 'That must be someone walking over my grave.'"

"Oh, *that* . . . yeah."

"Only it wasn't any 'someone.' It was a ghost. Trying to make contact."

Danny groaned when he remembered Joe's words. It was hopeless!

In fact, the ghost felt such contact more than the living person. It wasn't pleasant, either, Danny thought, flapping his hand about. Because instead of a chill, a ghost felt a nasty dull burning.

By now, Chester Adams was through talking. He gave Mike one last shake that sent him reeling against the side of the car. Jilly was still crying. Mike went to comfort her. Jilly howled all the louder. Even the two hoods leaning against their own car began to take pity on the kids.

"What goes on?" said Kelly.

"Mind your own—" began Chester.

Then his eyes met Roscoe's and his voice tailed off.

"Mind our own *what*, Fatso?" said Roscoe. "You wouldn't by any chance be telling us to mind our own *business*, would you?"

Chester blinked.

Jilly took heart.

"The big jerk! He's a big jerk, mister! He says he's gonna take half our candy money off us!"

"Yeah!" said Mike. "He says we steal it from Mom."

Roscoe grinned.

"And do you?"

"Yes, they do!" muttered Chester.

"We do *not!*" said Jilly.

"She *gives* it to us!" said Mike.

"She's always giving us money now!" said Jilly.

Roscoe's grin tightened. His eyes narrowed. He nudged Kelly, who was beginning to look impatient.

"Really? She must be very rich," said Roscoe.

"She is," said Chester. "*Now.* So now she gets drunker than ever. Then these creeps help themselves and—"

"Was I talking to *you*, Fatso? Shove off! So what if they did swipe it? You some kinda junior cop or something? Beat it!"

Roscoe's eyes were very hard now. Chester shrugged, then began to move away.

"I'll see you around!" he muttered at Mike and Jilly.

Jilly began to smile at Roscoe through her tears.

"You want some candy, mister?"

Danny groaned again. This was getting worse. Talk about jumping out of the frying pan into the fire!

"Hey, Jilly! Mike! Why don't you—"

Then Danny broke off, remembering they couldn't hear him.

Roscoe was grinning.

"No thanks, honey. . . . Uh—you say your mom's always *giving* you money now? She's *that* rich? Come *on!*"

He was looking at their clothes. Both Jilly's and Mike's were badly in need of a good cleaning. Not to mention mending. That had been one of Danny's jobs. When he was alive.

"It's true!" said Mike. "Ever since she got the money on account of Danny."

"Yeah!" said Jilly, in a low sad voice. Fresh tears sprang up in her eyes. "Danny got killed."

"Danny was our brother."

"If Danny was alive, *he'd* have helped us fight that creep!"

"Danny was always looking out for us."

"Always!" Now Jilly's tears were coming fast. Danny felt a sudden urge to grab her and hug her and swing her off her feet—around and around—the way she used to like him to do. "He—he used to play with us too," she added, just like she knew that Danny was there and even what he was thinking.

"Tough!" said Roscoe. "I bet all the money in the world wouldn't make up for Danny being killed."

"N-no!" sobbed Jilly.

"I hope your mom got a lot of money though, all the same," said Roscoe. "It's only fair."

"Sure!" said Mike, trying to look brave as he put an arm around Jilly. "The lawyer says she'll get a lot more, too. Comp— compin—"

"Compensation money?"

"Yeah!" said Mike. "That's what they call it."

Danny was nearly going crazy, wishing the kids would shut up and go.

"You live around here?" said Roscoe, gently.

"Yeah," said Mike. "Over there." He pointed across the street. "Just around the corner from the pool hall."

"Which—?"

It was Kelly who'd brought the questioning to an end. A sharp nudge made Roscoe wince and look at him angrily.

"You better be on your way, kids," said Kelly. "Before Fatso comes looking for you again."

When the brother and sister were out of earshot, Roscoe turned on Kelly.

"What was *that* all about?" he snarled. "I was thinking maybe there'd be some easy pickings there. Then *you* go and—"

"Sure! And so was I. Maybe it's worth looking into. But how many times do I have to tell you, Roscoe? You do *not* keep asking the same people questions. We can always find out more from someone else. Spread the questions *around*, OK? That way, no one remembers too much about who was asking."

"Well, sure. But, I mean, *kids*—well . . ."

"They have memories too, you know. Anyway— one job at a time. Come on! We've been hanging around here long enough."

Danny remained staring after the car, even when it had swung out of the lot and into the traffic. He was thinking that there were far more dangerous people around than neighborhood bullies like Chester Adams. He couldn't help remembering what Roscoe had said earlier about the gun. He wished he'd thought of memorizing the car's license-plate number.

Then Danny groaned again.

What could he have done with the number if he *had* memorized it? Who could he have reported it to? What *living person* could he have reported it to?

"Hey, Danny!"

He jumped.

Then he relaxed.

It was Joe Armstrong.

Joe looked just like any of the other people in the

street, as he hurried toward Danny. So did the girl with him. Joe was a burly young man with red hair and broad shoulders, dressed in jeans and a gray T-shirt with the words ARMSTRONG CONSTRUCTION stenciled across the chest. He looked a picture of solid health.

So did the girl. She was sixteen, with long blond hair and a deep tan. She was dressed perfectly for the hot weather in a thin red shirt and white shorts. They were in fact the clothes she'd been wearing the day she'd been knocked down and killed by a truck—nearly a year ago.

"Hi, Joe! Hi, Karen!"

For a few moments, Danny felt better. At least he could tell *these* two about his anxieties. They were ghosts. And at least ghosts can see other ghosts, hear other ghosts, touch and feel other ghosts.

But before Danny could tell them anything, Karen said: "Come on, Danny! We've been looking all over for you!"

"Why? What for?"

"Why?" said Joe, laughing. He was looking very excited, which was unusual for him. "Because Carlos has *done* it, Danny—that's why! He's *done* it!"

"What? Done what?"

"He's made it! He's made the big breakthrough! The one he's been talking about so much!"

"You mean—?"

"*Right!*" Karen grabbed his arm. "He's made contact. With a living person!"

"Hey! You aren't kidding me, are you?"

Joe looked grave all at once.

"Not over a thing like this, Danny!" He glanced over at the bank clock. "But he's going to give it the final test in exactly fifteen minutes, and he wants us to be there to see it. So—come on!"

3
Carlos

The streets they hurried through were crowded. It wasn't a very big or busy town. Yet ever since he'd become a ghost, Danny had grown aware of how crowded it really was. It was as if another two or three thousand people had come to live there.

He knew now what it was, of course. What he was seeing was the extra ghost population. He and his friends weren't the only ghosts hanging around. Joe had once explained this to him, and Danny thought about it now, as they hurried through the streets. . . .

"Not everybody who dies stays around as a ghost," Joe had said. "Otherwise it would be more than crowded."

"Who does stay then?" Danny had asked.

"People like you and me. People with problems. Heavy problems, connected with the living. Like you and your anxiety for your brothers and sisters. You feel you just can't go away completely while they still need you. Right?"

"Right! Though it's a fat lot of good I can do them now. Huh! . . . Anyway, what makes *you* hang around, Joe? Anxiety also?"

"Partly," the older ghost had said, grimly. "And partly determination. I just *have* to find out who killed me. My own murderer."

"You—you were *murdered?*"

"Yeah. I certainly didn't fall accidentally off the seventeenth floor of that building I was helping to construct. Only I still don't know who pushed me."

Then Joe had changed the subject by telling Danny about Karen Hansen and what made *her* stay around. Also their other friend, Carlos.

Karen was a bit like Danny. She was terribly anxious about her relatives—especially her father, who blamed himself for sending her on the errand that had ended in her death.

But Carlos was different. Carlos Gomez was some sort of electronics genius, even though he had been only thirteen when he was killed, ten months ago. Carlos just couldn't bear to leave the earth with some of his greatest experiments still unfinished. Like the experiment that had finished *him.* The word processor he'd been working on when he'd accidentally electrocuted himself.

"This experiment," said Danny, as they hurried along on their way to Wacko's. "Does it have anything to do with the one Carlos was working on when—?"

"The word processor. Yes. Trying to devise a circuit that would work on flashlight batteries. Minimum power supply—microcurrents—you know how he talks. But it's the *application* that concerns us now. The way it can be used. You'll see. . . . I hope!"

"So do I!" said Karen. "I mean—just think! He says he's figured out a way of operating the machine so he can talk to living people! I mean—wow!"

Danny was frowning.

He didn't know much about technical things. He personally wouldn't have dared hope that anything would come of this experiment. But Joe and Karen seemed convinced.

He brightened up.

If only they *could* get to talk to living people! Why, he'd be able to give good advice to his kid brothers and sisters. Maybe even straighten Mom up on a few points. And (here his grin broadened) give that creep Adams the fright of his life!

Yeah! They could—

He broke off.

They'd just rounded a corner of a quiet street of big old houses, lined with trees, and there was Carlos himself, doing a kind of war dance.

"*Come on come on come on!*" he babbled, without any pauses, hopping from foot to foot. "It's all set up. It's nearly five, and Wacko's up there waiting in his room. I got him to leave all the doors open, but there's no telling when his mom or one of his brothers might close one. Come on come on come *on!*"

Just as Joe looked very much alive with his sturdiness and Karen with her healthy glow, Carlos looked bubbling with life because of the way he moved.

His small compact body seemed to be dancing around them all the time as he ushered them up the driveway and through the front door, where the screen had been left propped open. With his black shaggy hair and sharp, darting, sparkling brown eyes, he reminded Danny of a small sheepdog he'd once seen on television. In this case, though, it was they— Joe, Karen and Danny—who were the sheep, to be driven now this way, now that.

Another big difference was that the sheepdog had done his work silently.

Not so Carlos. All along the hall and up the stairs, he kept up his chatter.

"It took me half an hour to get it through to him. 'Wacko,' I said, 'Wacko-Wacko-Wacko *please!* Forget all you ever read about ghosts! We *can't* walk through walls and solid doors. We have to slip through doors with living people when *they* go in and out. Or when they leave the doors open, or—' "

"You *told* him all this? Like now? Like you're telling *us?*"

"No, Joe. I'm sorry. Not exactly. You'll see. Hey, Karen, not that way, *this* way! Follow me."

The house was rambling as well as large. Danny had never realized how well-off Wacko Williams' parents must have been. The corridors had wall-to-wall carpeting. There were interesting pictures on the walls. The paintwork glowed. Everything looked clean. He couldn't help comparing it to the four-room dump in which he and his mother and brothers and sisters lived. Correction: in which he *had* lived with the other five.

"OK, OK! So here we are, here's Wacko's den, bedroom, laboratory, whatever. And here's my old friend, partner, assistant, call *him* what you like. But hey—from this day on, he's gonna be our *lifeline!* That's what we'll be calling him soon!"

The boy in the room didn't turn around as they filed in. After all, why should he? He couldn't hear Carlos or their murmured replies. All Wacko Williams could hear was the distant sound of his mother's voice, somewhere below. And the hum of the machine in front of him.

It was a long low room, with a bed at one end, half-hidden in a recess. There were drawers there, and bookshelves, and an open clothes closet, and a few chairs and throw rugs and posters—bedroom stuff. But at the other end, it was more like a workshop, with a huge table in front of the window, stretching right across the room. It was a table littered with tools and instruments and charts and what looked like half a million tiny electronic parts scattered around like confetti.

Only in the center was there anything like a clear space. And that was partly taken up by the machine.

"The word processor!" said Carlos, proudly.

To Danny it looked like a large gray typewriter

hooked up to a television screen. The screen had a faint greenish glow, like it was ready for action. Wacko was sitting back, with his long knobby fingers drumming the table.

"He's getting nervous," said Carlos. "Wacko always drums when he's nervous. I guess he's still wondering if he really did have that conversation with me earlier, or if he just dozed off and dreamed it."

Wacko looked at his watch. He was a thin, frail-looking black kid, with large serious eyes, fifteen years old. Danny remembered him well from school. Wacko—whose real name was Henry—Henry Williams—never had much to do with the other kids. Not because he was snooty. Simply because he was always thinking about his science problems. The only other kid he'd spent much time with had been Carlos. And that made sense. Wacko was a science whiz; Carlos had been a science *genius*. It had been a natural partnership.

"I told him five exactly," said Carlos, taking a peek at Wacko's watch. "Three minutes to go. So we'll wait. Experiments like this, you gotta be precise."

"And—and you can get messages across on word processors?" said Karen. "But how? How can *you* or any of us tap the keys? Our fingers wouldn't make the slightest impression on them, would they?"

"No! But remember one thing. This isn't just *any* word processor. This one—this one I know inside out, backward and forward. This one I worked on nearly a year, making modifications, adding special refinements. This one is extra sensitive to *me*."

"So?"

"Well—you know how we ghosts *can* make contact with people. By touching them. But how they can hardly feel it, even when we whack them really hard."

"Yes, but—"

"But they do feel *something*. A very minute vibration passes, even if they don't notice it much. Also you know—or maybe you guys don't, but Joe does—how some ghosts have the knack of attracting light floating things. Like particles of moisture—in a mist. Or swarms of gnats. Or snowflakes. Right, Joe?"

"Right. I can do it myself when I really concentrate."

"Right!" said Carlos. "And why? Because we ghosts are able to send out microwaves—that's why. And if we have access to instruments sensitive enough to pick up those microwaves—micro-micro-microwaves, to be precise—we can make things happen. Really interesting things. Meaningful things. Anyway, it's five o'clock—so—" he glanced at Wacko—"here we go!"

Wacko had suddenly crouched forward. There was a dark patch of sweat on his shirt, between the bony shoulder blades. Danny began to feel some of the tension himself.

Carlos was already peering over Wacko's right shoulder. Then Carlos reached out and spread his fingers in front of the keyboard. Now, for the first time, Carlos's body was still. Perfectly still.

Then the fingers began to dance. They didn't touch the keys. They just hovered, dancing, over them, as if he were typing in air.

"I'm trying," he said, softly, intently, "I'm trying to

put out just the right amount of microwave electricity to—to activate the circuits—like—like I was alive and—and able—to press the keys and—*aaah!*"

His long gasp was echoed by Karen.

Joe gave something between a grunt and a sigh.

Danny's eyes popped.

Wacko's whole body twitched.

And why?

Because a word had just been formed on the screen. One small, dumb, simple word. But mind-blowing in its effect.

"Hi!"

Wacko's twitching had turned to trembling. An eager trembling. He lifted his own hands and began hitting the keyboard.

"Hi! Carlos?"

Carlos made his fingers dance again, and the reply took shape.

> *"Affirmative. Dead on time—ha! ha!"*

"Hey, Carlos!" growled Joe. "Cut out the joking!"

"That's OK," said Carlos. "It's just to ease the tension. Wacko could get so uptight he might even pass out."

"He certainly isn't laughing," said Karen, not looking any too relaxed herself.

But Carlos was making more passes in front of the keyboard.

This time he wrote:

> *"There's no need for you to type your responses. We can hear you. You just talk. OK? I write: you talk."*

Wacko turned. His eyes were wide as he stared into what seemed like the thin air behind him.

"Uh—*we?*" he said. "You—you said *we*, Carlos? Who? Who's *we?*"

So began the strangest conversation that had ever taken place in that room—or any other room on earth.

4
The Ghost Squad

It didn't take Wacko long to loosen up after that.

As Carlos introduced the other three ghosts, Wacko began to act almost as if he could see them.

He'd never heard about Joe before, but he was glad to greet him.

"Any friend of Carlos is a friend of mine," he murmured, turning from the screen and nodding graciously.

But Danny he remembered very well. They'd only been separated by one grade at school. Wacko had been just as shocked as most of the kids when he'd learned of Danny's death, back in February. He also knew Buzz Phillips well—Danny's best friend and the boy who'd been with him when the old factory building they'd been exploring had collapsed.

"And I have to congratulate you, Danny," he said, staring at the spot where Carlos had told him Danny was standing. "Buzz once told me you got killed trying to save him."

"Aw—uh—yeah, well!" muttered Danny, squirming a little. "It was—well—uh—yeah!"

Carlos laughed.

"How'm I supposed to write *that* on the screen?"

As for Karen, this time it was Wacko's reaction that was amusing.

Of *course* he remembered the girl! He nearly leaped out of his chair when *her* name came up on the screen. She was a couple of years older than Wacko—or had been at the time of her death. But she'd been a cheerleader and voted by her class as Girl of the Year.

He scrambled to his feet and ran a hand over his hair, grinning with shy pleasure.

"How—how are you, Karen?"

"*Fine, Wacko!*" she got Carlos to reply on the screen. "*Under the circumstances . . .*"

By now they'd all grown so used to carrying on the ghost side of the conversation through Carlos and the machine that it was almost like speaking directly. Especially with Wacko showing such trust—*intelligent* trust—and never for a moment doubting that all this was really happening.

"But one thing puzzles me," he said, looking around uncertainly, then turning back to the screen.

"*What's that, Wacko?*"

"Well, you guys can see *me*, right?"

"*Affirmative.*"

"And you can all see each other, right?"

"*Affirmative.*"

"So—" Here Wacko looked embarrassed. "Well—I mean—like what with Danny being crushed by all those bricks and rubble and stuff. And—and Joe falling all that way. And Karen—" He sighed. "Well, you know—being hit by a truck—"

The ghosts grinned at each other and shook their heads.

"Tell him, Carlos," said Joe. "The kid's worried about whether we *would* look scary if he *could* see us."

"Yes," said Danny. "And especially tell him about Karen. Tell him she's just as—uh—good to look at— as ever."

Karen then proved something that all the professors in the world would never have guessed in a million years.

She proved that even ghosts can blush.

"Aw, come *on*, Danny!" she said—smiling.

When Carlos was through explaining to Wacko that ghosts always look the way they were before death had messed them up, wearing the clothes they felt best in at the time, Wacko seemed relieved.

And when Carlos added that even the clothes always look the way they did *before* death, even if the person died in an accident, his friend was totally at ease.

"Terrific! So now I know exactly what you're wearing, Carlos!"

"*Yeah?*" said Carlos, via the screen.

He glanced down at his old faded blue jeans and the bright yellow T-shirt with the blue logo across the front.

"Yeah! The yellow T-shirt, right? The Daisy Wheel shirt?"

Carlos grinned and transmitted the word *Affirmative!*

"So that's what that thing is called," said Joe, nodding at the logo.

It was like a wheel with a hub but no rim and about fifty spokes. At the center of the hub was a large letter G—originally for Gomez. At the end of each spoke was a letter of the alphabet or a number or some other symbol, like a dollar sign or a plus or a slash. Carlos had designed it himself and was very proud of it. One of his sisters had stenciled it on his shirt at the art school where she was a student.

"Every symbol *you'll* ever need for a word-processor printer is there," Carlos had once told Danny. "Except one. Nita left it out by mistake."

But in all the time Danny had known Carlos—as living person or ghost—the kid had never kept still long enough for Danny to check whether this was true or Carlos had been putting him on.

And so it was now.

Danny had just worked around to the letter *M* when Carlos suddenly swung around toward the door.

"I just knew you'd choose that shirt," Wacko was saying. "I—"

"Henry! Who *are* you talking to?"

All five of them—ghosts and living boy—got a nasty shock then.

They had been so engrossed in their conversation that only Carlos's sharp ears had heard Mrs. Williams approach the open door—and then it was nearly too late.

Wacko had the presence of mind to press the DE-LETE key and wipe out Carlos's last words.

"Uh—ah—*talking*, Mom?"

"Yes," she said, frowning down at him. "And look at you! Sweating. And with the air conditioner on high cool, too. . . . Are you feeling all right?"

"Oh—yeah—sure, Mom. Just busy—uh—working on the word processor."

Mrs. Williams sighed.

"You sure you aren't working *too* hard on it?"

"Well—uh—I—"

"I mean how long have you been *talking* to it?"

"It—it's nothing, Mom. Us scientists—we do kind of get all involved in our work."

"Seems like it. But sometimes you get *too* involved. Carlos was, when—*now* what's wrong?"

"Wrong, Mom?"

"You jumped just like you'd seen a ghost."

"Yeah—well. I guess it's mentioning Carlos."

"I'm sorry, son. I thought you'd gotten over it by now. But I was only going to say that that used to be *his* trouble. Now, you are taking care, aren't you? No danger of—?"

"No, Mom. Think I could ever forget, after what

happened? . . . Anyway, was there something you wanted?"

"Yes. Was it you who left the front door wide open, screen and all?"

"Aw, gee, yes! I guess it was."

"Well try not to do it again, huh? The hall was full of mosquitoes!"

When Mrs. Williams had left, shaking her head, Wacko got up and closed the door.

"Wow!" he said. "We'll have to be more careful in the future."

"*Affirmative!!*" Carlos wrote once again on the screen.

"Yes," said Joe. "And we'd better get down to business now, before anyone else interrupts." He looked around at his fellow ghosts. "And the business is this: Just how do we start putting all this to good use?"

"I've been thinking," said Karen, frowning slightly. "We still have one big problem. Mrs. Williams reminded me of it just now."

"What?" asked Joe.

"Well, just think about it. Suppose Wacko had told her the truth. Would she have believed him? No way! She'd have thought he really was sick!"

"Yeah, I guess you're right," said Carlos. "So?"

"So what happens if we get Wacko to go to our folks with messages? Like suppose I asked him to tell Dad it's OK. It wasn't his fault. That sure—he'd been nagging at me to go to the pharmacy for him. And that sure, I did stomp out in a bit of a temper. But what really made me run into the road without look-ing—"

Karen paused, shuddering at the memory. Then she lifted her head and went on: "Suppose I got Wacko to explain to Dad that it wasn't anything to do with me being mad. That it was seeing Rudy Pepper just leav-ing the store, and wanting to talk to him. That *that* was the reason."

"Well," said Danny, "if Wacko explains all that and tells your dad you yourself told him the true story— well, that should cheer him up, shouldn't. . . ." Danny trailed off. Then: "Uh-oh!" he said. "I see what you mean!"

"He'd look at Wacko like he really was wacky, right?" said Carlos. "Yeah, yeah, I see it too."

"Or worse," said Joe. "He might look at Wacko like he was just some plain nasty smart aleck, making a sick joke. I know my wife would think that if he went to *her* with a message from me!"

"Right!" said Karen. "So how can we get Wacko to convince our folks that we really *have* been in touch with him? That's the problem."

"Hey, you guys! You still there?"

Wacko was looking around, suddenly worried.

"Put him on hold," said Joe.

Hurriedly, Carlos transmitted the message: "*It's OK, Wacko. Keep your cool. We're in conference. We'll get right back to you.*"

Then Joe said: "It'll take some thinking out, I agree. But meanwhile there *are* some useful things he can be doing. More simple and straightforward things."

"Like what?"

"Well, he can tip people off about bad things being cooked up."

"Hey, yeah!" said Danny. "Like only this afternoon—"

But Joe was still talking.

"I mean all these months, apart from the trouble I've had solving my own problem, one thing has been bugging me horribly."

"What's that, Joe?" said Karen.

"Why, just being around and watching crimes being planned and committed. Or—or the wrong guys getting blamed. And me not being able to do anything about it."

"Right!" said Danny. "Only today—"

"It bugs me, too," said Carlos, doing a mini-war dance at the very thought. "Oh boy, does it bug me!"

"And me," said Karen. "It makes you feel so—so *powerless!*"

"Right!" said Joe. "But now we don't have to feel that way anymore. Now we *can* do something about it. Now we can help to clear up a whole bunch of mysteries and crimes in this town. With Wacko's help, we can stop a whole bunch of bad things from happening."

"Yeah! Wow!" Carlos was still dancing. "Like we were a new branch of the police department. A new squad. Like they have fraud squads and felony squads and—and—"

"That's it!" said Joe. "That's us! You, me, Karen and Danny! *The Ghost Squad!*"

5
First Assignment

After they'd told Wacko of the new development, and the excitement had begun to die down, the Ghost Squad hit another snag. It was nothing very drastic. Nothing to make them call the whole thing off.

But, like all newly formed organizations, the Ghost Squad soon discovered that there were a few bugs to clear out of the system before it could operate smoothly.

For instance, just as they'd been quick to see that they couldn't put Wacko to work on their personal problems right away, they now realized that their first strike against crime would have to be more carefully prepared than they'd expected.

Danny told them about Roscoe and Kelly. They all agreed that that should be their Number One major assignment. But then they started to work out their plan for Wacko's part in it—and hit the first snag.

"Don't *any* of you have an idea who those two guys are?" said Joe. "Their full names, where they live?"

The other ghosts shook their heads.

"They sounded like out-of-towners," said Danny.

Joe nodded, frowning.

Then he looked up, hopefully.

"You didn't by any chance get the license-plate number?"

Danny groaned.

"I thought of it. But no—I didn't figure it would be any use."

"I don't blame you, Danny," said Karen. "Who would have?"

"But you're sure they're not doing the job before Friday?" said Joe. "I mean really sure?"

"Positive. It all hangs on Mr. and Mrs. Hyman going to this dinner."

Joe sighed with relief.

"So that gives us four days. Four days to find out more about them. To collect some solid information for Wacko to give to the police." He shook his head again. "I wish we knew where they lived. At least *that!*"

Danny brightened.

"Well, probably we'll see them around town before

then. One of them did say something about asking more questions in the neighborhood."

He suddenly looked anxious.

"More questions about the Hymans?" asked Carlos.

"Huh—uh. . . . About where Mom and the kids live. I—I've got a nasty feeling that *they're* gonna be next on the list. After the Hymans . . . *my* house!"

Joe looked at him curiously.

"How's that, Danny?"

"The money. The insurance money. The kids started blabbing about it. And you should have seen the way that Roscoe latched on to it!"

Joe put a hand on his shoulder. A good, firm, solid and reassuring hand. Ghost to ghost.

"Don't worry. We'll nail them before that. . . ." Joe looked around at the others, suddenly brisk. "So here's what we do. We keep a sharp lookout for those two guys. And when we see them, we stick with them until we find out more about them. OK? We stick real close!"

"Like we were their own shadows," said Carlos. "You bet!"

"Better yet," said Karen. "Like *invisible* shadows!"

"Guys! You still around?"

Wacko was getting uneasy again.

Quickly, Carlos gave him a rundown on what they'd just decided.

As he stared at the screen, Wacko nodded.

"I understand," he kept saying, as the message flickered through. "I'm with you."

But he looked disappointed. He was swallowing hard.

"He's itching to get into action," said Carlos. "I can always tell with Wacko. Give him a good idea and he'll never rest until he's putting it into practice."

"We can get *him* to look out for Roscoe and Kelly as well," said Karen.

"No!" Joe was very emphatic. "Not yet. Remember, *he's* not invisible. They might get wise to him. And that Roscoe sounds like one very dangerous character." He smiled grimly. "Wacko wouldn't be very much use to the Ghost Squad *as* a ghost, would he?"

The others shook their heads. Carlos winced at the very thought.

Then Danny had another idea.

"One thing he *can* be doing—" He hesitated. "Uh—maybe."

"Yes? Go on."

"Well, it's personal really. But also a crime, in a way."

"So what *is* it?" cried Carlos, beginning to dance.

"Well, the reason I was staking out the parking lot in the first place was—well—I was waiting for Mike and Jilly. . . ."

Danny told them about Chester Adams.

Carlos and Karen knew Chester fairly well. Carlos growled and Karen looked angry when they heard about the bully's treatment of the little kids.

"So I thought maybe if we can get Wacko to—to sort of help out somehow—I mean—"

"That should be easy enough, Danny," said Joe. "I don't know the guy personally, but bullies are all alike. He won't like it when he realizes other people—people his own age—are wise to his little shakedown operation. Bullies scare easily. We'll get Wacko to give him a stern warning. Let him know he's being watched."

"By *us?*" said Karen.

"No. Just by *somebody*. Somebody who knows all the facts. That should be enough."

Carlos was already at work on the word processor.

Wacko was already nodding eagerly as he read the details.

"No problem!" he kept saying. "Easy! . . . I know the creep. . . . I'll have it out with him first thing tomorrow. In the school yard . . . Shaking down little kids! . . . The *jerk!*"

6
Setback
in the School Yard

Physically, Wacko Williams wasn't at his best the next morning. He had lain awake most of the night, his head seething with details and possibilities. Details of the strange conference that had taken place; possibilities of where it might lead, of the adventures and discoveries that would be certain to follow now that the Ghost Squad had made its breakthrough.

Mentally, however, he was very alert, very active, still seething. Normally reserved on the school bus— preferring quietly to mull over his various scientific problems—he deliberately struck up a conversation with Buzz Phillips that morning.

"Do you ever—uh—sort of get the feeling that someone you know who's dead is—uh—trying to get in touch with you, Buzz?"

Buzz was a tall, broad-shouldered boy, with a wide good-humored mouth and deep-set brown eyes. Now those eyes narrowed and the mouth tightened somewhat.

"That's a peculiar question, coming from you, Wacko. I thought you scientists didn't believe in spirits and things."

"Oh, I wouldn't say that! There's a lot of serious research work being done on ESP, you know."

"Uh-huh. . . ."

Buzz was still looking at him steadily, curiously.

"So, as I say, do you ever get the feeling—?"

"Are you trying to tell me *you* do, Wacko? I mean, is that why you're asking me? Because of—Carlos?"

Both boys had lost their best friends through sudden death. It had formed quite a strong bond of sympathy between them. But usually they avoided any direct mention of the subject.

Now that it had been raised openly, they both felt relieved. At least Wacko felt relieved, and the way Buzz's eyes had brightened, it looked as if he did, too.

"Sure!" said Wacko. "Definitely because of Carlos!"

He was grinning. Buzz looked a bit taken aback.

"You mean you think he's been—uh—trying to get in touch?"

"I'm pretty sure he has!" Then Wacko suddenly remembered himself and became sober. "But I was asking *you*. Uh—you know—if maybe Danny . . ."

Buzz sighed and shook his head. His expression became very sad.

"Look, if you don't want to talk about him—" said Wacko.

Buzz forced a smile.

"No—no, it isn't that. I don't mind talking about Danny. It's just that—well—I only wish he *would* try and get in touch."

"You don't ever have a feeling maybe he's still around?"

"Not really. I guess you're remembering about the dreams he used to have. The dreams that seemed to foretell the future."

Wacko nodded. It had been something he used to jeer at—looking at it from a strictly scientific angle.

"Yeah. You used to call yourselves—uh—Time Explorers Incorporated. That it? . . . With Danny doing the dreaming and you doing the interpreting. You used to claim some pretty spectacular results, as I recall."

"We used to *get* some pretty spectacular results!" Buzz sighed again. "But me, I never dream. And I guess if Danny's spirit, ghost, whatever—I guess if it was anywhere around, that's where it would try to make contact. In my dreams. Which I don't have."

Wacko was going to tell him that it was a scientific fact that everybody dreamed. That it was just that some people could never remember dreaming. But Buzz looked so sad now—almost annoyed with himself, too—that Wacko decided to drop the subject.

When the kids got off the bus and started drifting or striding toward the main entrance of the school,

Wacko hung back. Usually he was one of the striders, anxious to get to work, but today of course he had an important mission to undertake first.

He began to leaf through one of his books, pretending to look for something but really keeping a watch on the gate.

He didn't have long to wait. The downtown bus arrived a few minutes later, and Chester was one of the first to get off.

"Chester Adams."

The bully looked surprised at being greeted by one of the older kids.

"Oh—yeah—hi, Wacko!" he said, with an oily squirming grin.

"My name is Henry," said Wacko, coldly but politely. "To *you* it is, anyway. And I'd like a few words with you, if I may."

No longer grinning but still feeling flattered, Adams said: "Why, yes, sure—uh—Henry. What about?"

Another busload of kids had just driven up.

"It's rather confidential. Why don't we step around the side of the building, where we won't be interrupted?"

"How d'ya like that guy? Always polite, always was polite, too darned polite for the likes of this creep!"

Not Wacko, not Chester, not any of the kids entering the yard heard this, even though it was delivered in a high, excitable voice. Only the ghosts of Danny, Joe and Karen heard Carlos's comment.

"One thing about being polite, though," said Karen,

as the Ghost Squad followed the two boys around the corner. "It always has a steadying effect on jerks like Chester Adams. They're never quite sure how to take it."

"So long as he gets the *message!*" said Danny.

"Oh, he will!" said Joe. "Listen. It's just about to be delivered."

"OK," Wacko was saying. "This'll do." He glanced around. As far as he could tell, he and Chester were alone, over by the garbage cans outside the school kitchen. "And what I have to say won't take long."

"Good!" said Chester. "The bell will be ringing soon and I'm already in trouble with—"

"You're already in trouble—period. With more than your homeroom teacher or anyone else in this place."

"Huh?"

The bully's mouth hung open slackly.

"Yes. And if you go on shaking down those little Green kids, you'll be in *real* trouble, real police-type trouble. OK?"

Chester's mouth still hung open. His face was turning red.

"Whu—what little green kids? This some kinda joke?"

"Not green the color, jerk! Green the *name*. Danny Green's kid brother Mike and his sister Jilly!"

Chester's mouth suddenly closed. His eyes went smaller than ever—small and mean.

"Oh—oh!" groaned Carlos. "Watch it, Wacko! I

don't like the way this is shaping up—no, sir!—not at *all!*"

For now the bully was obviously beginning to feel more like his old self. All at once he seemed to realize that although Wacko was a year older, he was a couple of inches shorter and a good fifteen pounds lighter.

"Now see here—*Wacko!*" he said, deliberately emphasizing the name and advancing slowly and heavily. "You don't want to go listening to any old lies any old riffraff like those Green kids decide to tell you."

"It wasn't them. So—" said Wacko, beginning to back off.

"So who else *could* it have been?" sneered Chester, still advancing.

"Oh, gosh!" said Karen. "This is where politeness isn't going to be much use, after all!"

"The dummy shouldn't even have *tried* to be polite!" howled Carlos. "He shoulda told him in front of a *crowd!*"

"So—" said Chester, giving Wacko a final shove with the flat of his hand, "don't listen to lies like that no more in the future, or you might get hurt. Heh! heh!"

The laugh came with the crash. The crash came with Wacko's tripping over one of the garbage cans.

The can was empty, but it hadn't been one hundred percent clean. Wacko's sleeve was smeared with salad dressing. His jeans at the back felt suddenly tacky, and he realized he was sitting on a piece of rejected lemon meringue pie.

"Hey, Wacko!" Chester Adams called over his shoulder as he swaggered away. "What're you doing with that garbage can? Think you're a raccoon or something? Heh! heh! heh!"

Maybe he wouldn't have laughed so freely if he'd been able to see the ghost of Carlos Gomez just then, prancing around him with fury and aiming useless phantom punches at his nose.

As for Wacko, suddenly he felt the whole weight of his near-sleepless night as he dragged himself to his feet. His face wore a hurt as well as a haggard look.

"I don't know whether you guys are with me or not, right now!" he muttered. "But if you are, we're gonna have to talk about this later, when we have access to the word processor. There's *got* to be a better way!"

7
Wacko Makes a Request

The Ghost Squad knew exactly what Wacko meant when he talked about seeing them "later."

Yesterday they had agreed to get together again the next afternoon at three-thirty in Wacko's room.

"What if we should get lucky though, and spot Roscoe and Kelly, and we're still following them at that time?" Carlos had asked. "What then?"

"Good question," said Joe. He thought a moment. Then: "OK. Tell Wacko this. That if for any reason we can't make it at three-thirty, he must try again exactly one hour later."

"And if we're still on the trail?"

"One hour after that, and so on, until we do make contact."

46

So it had been agreed, with Wacko promising to do his best either to leave the doors open again or at least to be at the front door himself.

"I can pretend to be letting myself in sort of slowly," he'd said. "Like I was undecided about something."

"So long as you give us time to slip through!" the message had flickered back.

"Yeah. But listen, guys. You *sure* you can't sneak in through cracks and chinks and things? Being ghosts and all? I mean it *would* help, you know."

Then Carlos had explained that yes, they could. But only with great difficulty and very unpleasant side effects.

"So we can use it only in extreme emergencies—repeat—extreme emergencies. OK?"

Wacko had nodded, and repeated that he'd do his best.

But, as it turned out, there was no need for any special emergency procedure that day. All Tuesday morning and early afternoon—ever since witnessing the setback in the school yard—the Ghost Squad had been patrolling the town without any luck. There was no sign of Roscoe and Kelly.

"Well, no sweat," said Joe, after they'd made a final check at the railroad station parking lot. "It's only Tuesday. And maybe we'll spot them later, after our meeting with Wacko." He glanced at the bank clock. "Hey! It's three-fifteen. Let's move!"

Wacko was at the front door when they arrived. He

was looking very nervous as he lingered there, with the screen open.

"What are you standing there for, Henry?" his mother called from inside.

"Oh—I—I think I saw a hummingbird, Mom. I'm —uh—interested in the way they hover. The aerodynamics aspect."

Carlos grinned as he passed through.

"I taught him that trick," he said. "When parents ask too many questions, snow 'em with scientific words. It never fails."

It must have worked this time, anyway. There was no reply from Mrs. Williams.

"If you're here, you guys," murmured Wacko, "*please* get inside quick. I'll count to four."

"Did you say something, Henry?"

"No, Mom. Just kind of singing to myself."

Wacko sighed, shut the screen door and went upstairs. At least he didn't have to worry about his room door, already standing open.

The Ghost Squad went in a few steps ahead of him.

He walked over to the word processor and switched on.

Immediately, the following message flashed onto the screen: "*Hi, Wacko! All present. You can shut the door now.*"

"Right," said Wacko, when he'd done that, "so let's get right to this morning's problem."

Carlos only had time to begin: "*We were sorry—*"

"So was *I!* And I've been thinking. And you know what I think?"

"Oh-oh! He's still sore," said Carlos. "When Wacko's sore it's best to tread carefully."

He made a single delicate pass at the keybroad. A single delicate message resulted:

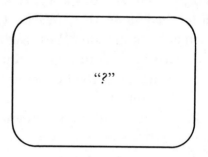

Wacko nodded grimly and said: "What I think is if this is gonna work out, I'll need assistance, OK?"

The ghosts looked at each other.

"I mean, you saw what happened this morning," said Wacko.

"He has a point," said Joe, "but—"

"And—hey!—there's another thing," said Wacko. "There'll be less chance of my mother getting suspicious. About me talking to myself. If I had an assistant with me. Right?"

"Tell him to be quiet a minute," said Joe. "While we think."

"*Your request is being considered,*" Carlos flashed onto the screen. "*Please hold.*"

"What worries me," said Joe, "is can we risk letting

too many living people in on the secret? I mean would we be able to trust them?"

"Maybe we should ask if he has any special person in mind," said Karen.

"Hey—yes!" said Danny, suddenly thinking of one very special person.

"OK," said Joe. "Go ahead, Carlos. Ask him."

When Carlos had done that, Wacko had replied without a moment's hesitation: "Yes. Buzz Phillips!" Then Danny's face broke into a grin, Karen nodded approvingly and Carlos breathed easier.

Joe still looked doubtful.

"You think he'd be—well—sympathetic enough?" he asked Danny.

"Positively!"

"I mean in the sense that he wouldn't laugh at Wacko when he raised the subject?"

"No problem!"

"He's also smart," said Carlos. "To understand about the word processor, I mean. His father's a science teacher, you know. A college professor."

"OK, Carlos. Just to make sure Wacko knows what he's doing, ask him, One: Why Buzz Phillips? And Two: Has he mentioned this to him already?"

Wacko's reply was prompt and firm: "Taking the second question first—no, I haven't mentioned it to Buzz yet. Not directly. But I did sort of sound him out, and I'm sure he'd jump at the chance of contacting Danny again."

"You bet!" said Danny. "Me too!"

"Quiet, Danny. Let's hear the answer to the first question."

"And as to why I've suggested Buzz," Wacko was saying, "well—mainly it's because this morning's disaster taught me one thing. If I'm going to do the legwork as well as being your mouthpiece, it's probably going to take me into some pretty tough spots. *Physically* tough!"

He paused and looked slowly around at where he guessed they'd be standing.

"OK? So look at me. *I'm* not built like a quarterback. I'm in no shape to handle even a kid like Chester Adams. I'm just not that type. But Buzz Phillips is."

"That's true," said Karen. "*He'd* have taken care of Chester."

"So how about it, guys?" Wacko was continuing. "May I at least invite Buzz around here? Say tomorrow at this time? At least to give it a try, see how he likes the idea?"

The Ghost Squad didn't take long.

Joe was still a little reluctant.

"I guess I'm getting old. I like to feel my way into a new situation more slowly. But—well—you three know the kid better than I do. How about it?"

"I think it's a terrific idea!" said Danny. Then he frowned. "But—well—I'm biased."

"It's certainly obvious that Wacko needs *some* help," said Karen. "I say we could do a lot worse than give Buzz a try."

"Hey—and yeah!" said Carlos, beginning to hop

about. "I just thought of something. I mean suppose Wacko was to get sick and had to go into the hospital a day or two for allergy tests again. Well then—wow!— what would we do for a contact *then?*"

Joe looked startled.

"I never thought of that!"

"Yeah. Me either," said Carlos. "But if Buzz comes in on this—no problem. Wacko would just tell his mom that Buzz was working with him on the word processor. Then he'd ask her to let Buzz have access to it, to run some checks or something. I mean that's what we did once when he *was* hospitalized and I was still alive."

Joe was nodding.

"OK. I guess that settles it. Tell him yes, Carlos. He can go ahead. But tell him to break it very cautiously to Buzz, and only in our presence, in this room, to-morrow, at three-thirty."

"Affirmative!" said Carlos, already getting busy in front of the word processor.

8
Chester Shows His Hand

That evening, the Ghost Squad did get lucky. It got very lucky. The trouble was—it also got very unlucky.

And it both cases, it was thanks to Danny.

Because he was the only member of the squad who'd ever had a good look at the two hoods, it was left to him to choose where to search. Naturally, he tended to concentrate on the area around the railroad station, where he'd first seen Roscoe and Kelly. After all, that was where the hoods' first hit was scheduled to take place, at the Hymans' jewelry store. And possibly their second, too.

But something else was on Danny's mind that evening. He was still worried about Chester Adams, and the danger Mike and Jilly were in.

"OK," he kept telling himself. "So if Buzz does team up with Wacko tomorrow, that problem will probably be taken care of. But suppose for some reason Buzz doesn't join Wacko. What then?"

It seemed to Danny that *then* the danger would be greater than ever. Because, sure as anything, the bully would still be out to get Mike and Jilly, really believing they had finked on him to Wacko.

And tomorrow was tomorrow—Buzz or no Buzz. And there was still tonight.

So with this worry nagging at him, he tended to lead the squad around places where the bully might go to track the kids down.

Which was why, just after nine o'clock, the Ghost Squad was standing outside The Railroad Diner for what must have been the fifth or sixth time in the last two hours. The Railroad Diner was owned and operated by Chester's parents. Danny knew his kid brothers and sisters were still playing on the street just outside their house—way past the time they should have been. So he kept checking to make sure that Chester was at home and hadn't taken it into his head to go out looking for them.

There wasn't much that he or any of the other ghosts could have done if Chester had gone out in search of revenge. But Danny just had to keep checking, all the same.

"They work pretty hard, I'll say that," said Karen, looking in on the small busy room, with its red and white checkered plastic table covers, and the counter where Mr. Adams was dishing out some steaming food.

"Uh—what? Who?" said Danny.

"Mr. and Mrs. Adams. It's a pity that fat jerk doesn't give them more help. All he seems to do is come in and help himself to another can of Coke or piece of pie. Just look at him!"

Karen looked disgusted, but Danny felt pleased. To see Chester Adams eating or drinking up the family profits was a fine sight just then. It meant Mike and Jilly were safe for the time being.

"He's spoiled," said Carlos. "They ruin him, his mother especially. The only child."

"Yes," said Karen. "Plus they had him late in life. They're old enough to be his grandparents really. Which is all the more reason why he should lend them a hand. The creep!"

"Excuse me for interrupting," said Joe. "But are we a bunch of social workers or are we a crime-fighting squad? We're supposed to be looking for—"

"Hey! For Roscoe and Kelly, right?" said Danny, suddenly alert. "Well there they *are*, right there, just going up to the counter! They must have walked right past us while we were looking in the window."

"You sure it's them?"

"*Positive!*" said Danny.

They were dressed differently. Roscoe was wearing a black lightweight cotton sweater; Kelly had on a plain blue blazer. But Danny was in no doubt as he watched them saying something to Chester behind the counter and Chester shrugging and pointing to his father, still busy with the customers ahead of them.

"That's Roscoe, the one leaning forward and talking to Chester."

"Yeah—and telling him something the creep doesn't like to hear," said Carlos.

"Probably asking why *he* won't serve them," said Karen.

"But the other one seems to be telling Roscoe to cool it," said Joe. "Anyway, let's not just stand here *guessing*. As soon as the door opens again, Danny and I will go in and get close enough to hear them. Karen, Carlos—you two wait outside. Then if Danny and I don't make it through the door fast enough when they leave, you can follow them to their car or whatever. OK?"

The other two nodded. Danny and Joe took up their positions by the door. Almost at once, an elderly lady came along and started fumbling with the door handle. Following *her* in was easy.

Roscoe and Kelly were placing their orders when the two ghosts moved up behind them. Chester had gone through the doorway leading back into the house, looking glad to get away.

"That your kid?" Roscoe snapped, as Mr. Adams wrote down his order.

Mr. Adams nodded. He smiled weakly. He was a thin pasty-faced little man, with a wisp of gray hair flattened across the top of his bald head.

"Sure is, sir! Fine boy!"

"Oh yeah?"

Roscoe sounded ready to give him an argument on that score, but Kelly gave a stealthy tug at his sleeve.

"Two specials with french fries, Ma," said Mr. Adams, turning to the kitchen entrance, where the fat figure of Mrs. Adams could be seen bending over the heat and the glare of the stove.

"Listen, Roscoe!" muttered Kelly. "Cool it, OK? Just cool it! The last thing we need is to attract attention."

"Be ready in five minutes, gents," said Mr. Adams, coming back. "Why don't you take a seat, and I'll bring it across to you? . . . Yes, Mrs. Gromek?"

Roscoe looked ready to take offense even at those mild words. After lingering longer than necessary and giving the next customer a nasty look, he finally joined his partner at a table by the window.

"It's a dump!" he muttered. "You want us to get food poisoning? That it?"

"We didn't come here for the cuisine, remember? Now for Pete's sake shut up, Roscoe, and keep your eyes skinned. This is perfect—just perfect—for our purpose."

Danny and Joe, standing over the two unsuspecting hoods, exchanged glances.

"I wonder what purpose that would be?" murmured Joe.

"Perfect for a stakeout, yeah!" said Roscoe, with a sudden laugh. "But I wouldn't like to bet on the steaks!"

Kelly smiled.

"Don't worry. Come Saturday we'll be eating in style. . . . Meanwhile"—he turned to the window— "let's see if we can find out just when that patrol car goes by. In these hick towns, it's usually the same times every night. And if we know *that*, we can plan accordingly."

"Why worry?" sneered Roscoe. "So what if some hayseed cop does stumble across us. Wanna bet who'd win, if it comes to a shoot-out?"

"Keep your voice down, dummy!" Now Kelly's eyes were hard. Even Roscoe had to look away. Then: "Yes," said Kelly, leaning forward and speaking softly but very emphatically. "I *will* bet. *They* would win. Because you will not—repeat *not*—be carrying a gun. Clear?"

"Sure, Kelly, sure! Hey, I was only kidding!"

"Well, shut up and watch. . . . *Gee! This looks good!*" Kelly was smiling as Mr. Adams came up with their plates. "It really does!"

And it really did. The Railroad Diner always gave good value, as Danny knew. In fact, it was almost too much for him to take, just looking at those rich glistening brown steaks and crispy golden french fries.

"What's the matter, Danny?" asked Joe, grinning. "Still getting the feeling you're hungry?"

Danny smiled sadly.

"I don't know. . . . It's been weeks now. But from time to time—well—you know how it is."

Joe nodded. He'd long since gotten over this difficulty. The fact was, ghosts don't need food. Not even

58

ghost food. But for a time, the new ghost's memory will persuade him that he *is* hungry.

"Try and think of something else," he said.

"I am!" said Danny, grimly.

Turning from the tantalizing food, he had just caught sight of Chester again.

The boy had returned to the counter, probably to get another Coke. But at that moment Mr. Adams had gone back into the kitchen, leaving the counter—and the cash register—unattended.

"Did you see *that?*" asked Danny.

"What?"

"That creep! Just then!"

"What? Doing what?"

"Dipping into the drawer of the till, that's what!"

"You sure?"

"Certain! Look at the way he's keeping his right hand in his pocket. That's the hand that just plucked out a bill. . . . Hey! Excuse me, Joe. I'm just going to have to see what he does with it!"

9
Trapped!

Chester was already moving away.

"Well, don't—"

Before Joe could finish, Danny had dashed across the room and around the back of the counter. He was just in time to slip through the doorway with Chester.

He needn't have rushed, though. Chester himself was in such a hurry to get away with his loot that he left the door open behind him. And even as he was going up the stairs, that boy couldn't resist pulling the bill out of his pocket.

"Twenty!" he murmured gleefully. "Beautiful!"

"Thief!" growled Danny. "And *that's* why you were so quick to accuse Mike and Jilly! You think everyone else is just as crooked as you!"

Chester went straight ahead at the top of the stairs to a room directly opposite. It had a fancy plastic notice on the door: *Chester*, in curly letters encircled with different colored flowers and little chickens and baby rabbits.

Danny couldn't help grinning.

"I bet you wouldn't like the guys at school to know about the baby sign on your door, creep!"

He was still sticking close, as Chester entered the room.

Then he got a mild shock.

"Guess what I brought for your supper *tonight*, Theodore!" Chester was saying.

Danny looked around. The room was very well furnished, with a thick carpet and matching drapes and bed covers. It was also very untidy, with toys and games of all kinds spilling from the shelves and littering the floor. Most of these things looked new, like Chester had played with each one for only a hour or so before tossing it aside.

But that wasn't what interested Danny so much, just then. He was curious to know who this Theodore was. Chester was an only child, so it couldn't be a brother. And Danny had never heard of him owning a pet.

Then, as Chester leaned over the bed, Danny gasped.

Lying there, between the sheets, with its head on a pillow, was—*a teddy bear!*

Danny couldn't believe his eyes. Or his luck.

After all, Chester was fourteen years old!

And if the guys at school ever got to hear about this, that creep's life wouldn't be worth living. The sign on the door was *nothing* compared to this!

The grin began to spread across Danny's face again. Then he frowned.

Chester had turned the grubby old one-eyed bear over, and his fingers were probing its back.

"Supper, Theodore! How about a nice fat twenty-dollar bill?"

Danny bent closer. As Chester began to push the now neatly folded bill through a slit in the bear's back, Danny caught a glimpse of more green paper.

"That's a good bear! Eat it up nice!"

Carefully, Chester plucked at the original stuffing, covering his stash with it so that anyone accidentally spotting the slit would never notice what else was inside.

"Now just you digest *that*, while Chessy-wess gets ready for bed!"

Again the grin crept across Danny's face.

"*Chessy-wess!*" he jeered. "Oh boy! Wait till I tell Wacko about this!"

Chester was taking off his clothes and letting them drop on the rug. He didn't bother to pick them up or fold them.

"That figures, you slob!" muttered Danny, still grinning. "Now hurry up and get into some pajamas and go brush your teeth so I can slip out with you and tell Joe and the others what I've just—uh—"

Danny's jaw dropped.

Either Chester had already been to the bathroom, or he wanted to get into bed quickly and pretend to be fast asleep in case his parents found out about the missing money.

With a gleeful "Night-night, Theodore!" the bully had switched off the light and snuggled down between the sheets, hugging his bear.

Danny turned quickly—then groaned.

The darkness didn't bother him. One of the advantages of being a ghost was that you could see much better in the dark than when you were alive. It wasn't like broad daylight, but even in the darkest room or outdoors on the blackest night, a ghost's eyes could still make out the shapes and positions of various objects.

This ghost's eyes didn't have to stare very hard to realize that Chester had closed the bedroom door very firmly. It wasn't even slightly ajar, for Pete's sake! And already the jerk was beginning to breathe deeply and steadily—really settled in for the night!

"Danny! Where are you?"

Danny was just taking a look at the window, through a gap in the drapes, when Joe's voice made him turn.

"Joe?"

"Who else? Where are you?"

The voice didn't sound very close.

"In here. In Chester's room. There's—there's a dumb sign on the door."

There was a brief pause. Then: "Uh—yeah! I see it. Hey, Danny! Don't tell me you're shut *in!*"

"I—I'm sorry, Joe. He's gone to bed. I didn't expect—"

"Aw, Danny! How *could* you? Roscoe and Kelly are getting ready to go! How about the window?"

"I was just looking, Joe. It—it isn't any good. It's open, but the screens are in the way."

"OK, OK!" Joe sounded like he was fighting hard to keep his temper. "Well, listen, Danny—can you *see* all right?"

"Pretty well, but—"

"So take a good look around. Is there anything ready to overbalance? If there is, see if you can make it fall down, OK? It might just scare him enough to jump out of bed and go running for his parents."

Danny grunted. He began prowling around, over by the shelves. They looked like his best bet.

"You know what I mean, Danny, don't you?"

"Sure, Joe. I'm looking. . . ."

Danny did know what Joe meant. He knew that a skillful, patient ghost could sometimes use his store of micro-energy to affect solid objects, if those objects were in a delicate enough state of balance. A glass teetering at the edge of a shelf. A coat hanging by a thread on a hook. A boulder poised at the crumbling margin of a cliff. That sort of thing.

In such conditions, a ghost's energy could have an effect. That tiny extra tilt could cause the glass to fall, or the coat to drop off the hook, or the boulder to go bounding down, taking half the cliff with it.

Then living people sometimes got a shock. Some were quick to laugh and say it must have been the vibration from a passing truck or aircraft. Others got closer to the truth—and talked about poltergeists.

Danny looked around anxiously. He'd never tried anything like that yet, and he was wondering if he'd have the skill.

Even if he did find something ready poised.

"Any luck?"

"No—I guess—"

Danny had been prodding at a pair of binoculars at the edge of one of the shelves, half on, half off. But they were still too firmly anchored by their own weight.

"OK. Don't panic. Keep looking. I'll see if I can find anything out here."

Ten minutes must have gone by. Danny tried an empty Coke can that lay on its side on the night stand; the bulb in the lamp, which looked a bit wobbly; a box of BB pellets that had been put down carelessly on top of another box on the shelf. (Boy, what a rattle they'd make! he thought.)

But it was no good.

It looked like he'd be trapped there until morning.

Unless Chester had to get up to go to the bathroom.

He glared at the snoring figure.

"I mean, all the Coke you've been drinking," he said aloud, "you'd think you'have had to go *before* getting into—"

The almighty crash, somewhere beyond the closed door, made even Danny jump.

Chester gave a yell and sat bolt upright.

Voices began to call up the stairs.

"What was *that?*"

"*Chester!*"

Then Joe's voice, closer, above the sound of thudding footsteps.

"Get ready, Danny!"

The door burst open just as Chester switched on the light.

"Momma!" he cried.

"Son!"

"What happened?" asked Danny, as he slipped past the bulky figure of Mrs. Adams.

"Never mind that now!" said Joe, looking annoyed. "Come on! They might—just *might*—still be around!"

Danny didn't need to ask who "they" were.

But Roscoe and Kelly were long gone. The only customer left was Mrs. Gromek, who was standing by the counter, waiting to pay her bill. The street door was closed. Joe stamped with impatience.

"What was it?" Mrs. Gromek asked, as Mr. Adams came back into the room.

"The durnedest thing!" said the little man. "Bathroom cabinet fell off the wall. I'd been meaning to fix that loose screw for weeks, but I never figured it was as loose as *that!*" He sighed. "What with—uh—certain items mysteriously disappearing, and now this—I sometimes get to thinking the place is haunted."

Danny looked at Joe, grinning.

Joe scowled back.

"It wasn't all *that* easy! And it isn't all *that* funny!"

"Sorry!"

"Ah, forget it! Let's just make sure we leave when the old lady leaves, that's all!"

They did leave, less than a couple of minutes later. But there was nobody waiting for them outside.

"I guess Karen and Carlos had no choice but to go right after them," said Danny, miserably. "I really am sorry, Joe."

Joe clapped him on the shoulder. He was looking more like his usual patient self.

"I said forget it, Danny. We all make mistakes. And this is exactly why I told Karen and Carlos to keep watch outside. They're a couple of experienced ghosts. They'll be following those guys right now— this very minute—and they won't come back without bringing the information we need. Even if it takes them all night. You'll see!"

10
Crisis!

Well, Joe was right about one thing. It certainly did take the other two all night.

Joe wasn't worried about this. In fact, as soon as it became clear that he and Danny were in for a long wait, he seemed relieved.

"It's obvious what's happened," he said, when the bank clock flicked over to 11:00.

"Oh?"

"Sure! They've followed Roscoe and Kelly home. They must have stuck real close to those two guys when they left the diner. Then, as soon as they got in their car, Carlos and Karen would jump aboard."

"They must have moved faster than I did," said Danny, still embarrassed at goofing things up. "I mean, following somebody through a *car* door takes some—"

"Not necessarily," said Joe. "Maybe they didn't go inside at all. They could simply have sat on the trunk. Or on the hood. Don't forget, they're *ghosts*, Danny. No slipstream's going to blow *them* off, however fast the car's going. And even if they sat on the roof with their legs over the windshield, *they're* not going to obstruct the driver's view!"

Danny laughed, for the first time since they'd come out of the diner.

"I keep forgetting!"

"Yeah. So I notice. . . . Hey, but don't worry. You'll get used to it. Anyway, I hope they did ride on the outside. It wouldn't do for them to have gone all the way to those guys' place and then get shut up in the car. It could easily happen if they weren't fast enough slipping out."

"Maybe that's what *has* happened," said Danny. "Maybe that's why it's taking them so long."

"I doubt it. Karen and Carlos both know the score. They're both fast movers. No," said Joe. "The way I figure it is this. Those guys are out-of-towners, right?"

"Right."

"So that means they live someplace at least six or seven miles away. Possibly as much as twenty or thirty. OK. So Karen and Carlos take a good look at the house—its number, which street, like that—so that we'll have enough hard information to pass on to the police. Then they have to make their own way back."

"On *foot?*"

"Whatever way they can. Hopefully they can grab another ride. But it could take hours."

"Yeah, but supposing they lose their way?"

"Danny, you worry too much! D'you think Carlos and Karen won't have thought of that on the way out? They'll have been checking every mile of the route—every landmark, every road sign. Carlos will, anyway."

Danny nodded.

"Yeah. Carlos is one bright kid. Not like me!"

"Stop putting yourself down, Danny! If it hadn't been for you keeping your ears open, we'd never have been on the track of those guys in the first place! Anyway, there's no point hanging around second-guessing. Let's put the time to good use and give you some practice in getting finely balanced objects to move. You need it."

"You can say that again!"

"OK. So I'll show you some of the most finely balanced objects in the living world. Any ghost can get these to move the way he wants, if he really sets his mind to it. Follow me."

They didn't go far. Just over the railroad tracks and down a slope, to where a muddy old creek ran alongside the power plant fence. Beyond the fence the bright arc lamps that lit up the yard cast some of their light onto the creek itself.

Joe pointed to one of the stray beams.

"There you go," he said. "See 'em? Swarming in that beam?"

"Gnats?"

"Right! Now watch this. . . ."

Joe went and stood at the edge of the creek in the cloud of gnats. If he'd been a living person, they would have had a good supper off him. As it was, they didn't seem to notice him. Which made sense, Danny thought. What with Joe being a ghost and them being living creatures and all.

Joe had closed his eyes. He stood very still—as still as only a ghost can.

Then Danny gasped.

The swarm of gnats seemed to become aware of Joe. Or at least become attracted to the space he occupied. The swarm thickened, shrank, concentrated. Still vibrating, each tiny member drew closer to its neighbor until Joe's features were obscured and all that could be seen was a seething grayish cloud—*in the shape of a man!*

"Pow!"

Joe's breath came out with a sudden explosion as he walked out of the cloud. The gnats stayed together in the man-shape for a second or two, then began to spread and hover: just a regular swarm of gnats again.

"How about that?" said Joe, laughing.

"But—how—?"

"Concentration," said Joe. "You concentrate your mind on the gnats. You shut everything else out but them. And somehow—well—that energy communicates with their energy, and you act as a sort of magnet. It's the same sort of thing that happens with

Carlos and the electronic energy in the word processor. On a much cruder scale, of course."

"Do you think *I'll* ever be able to do that?"

"The gnats? Sure! All it takes is practice. Why don't you try it now? Just one finger at first. Just stick your finger into that swarm and concentrate. Go on!"

Danny spent hours that night, practicing the technique. He made very slow progress at first, and they had to keep breaking off to go back to the street outside the diner to see if Carlos and Karen had returned.

But Joe was very patient.

And when Danny had graduated from getting the gnats to swarm around his index finger, to his whole hand, and then to the arm all the way up to the elbow, Joe clapped Danny on the back.

"Terrific! Now you really are getting somewhere!"

"Yeah! It's quite a trick!"

Then Joe became very serious.

"More than a trick, Danny. It's something that may come in very handy some day. I mean, just think. Suppose some living person had been passing by. What would he have seen?"

"Not *us*, that's for sure."

"No—*but a swarm of gnats in the shape of a man?* Or—*gnats swarming in the shape of a hand or an arm?* How d'you think he'd have taken *that?*"

"He'd have been scared, I guess."

"Darned right he would! In fact, he *would* think he'd seen a ghost, is my guess. But whatever he thought it was, he'd have seen something caused by us. And that's one way of communication between the living and the—uh—*us*. Right?"

Danny nodded. He suddenly felt excited.

"Right! You mean the Ghost Squad—?"

"I mean the Ghost Squad can use as many ways as we can think of to get messages across. I mean suppose something went wrong with the word processor? A power outage, a burned-out part, anything. We need a backup system, right? Or suppose Wacko was really badly sick, or got *killed*, even?"

"Yes. I see what you're getting at. Or if Carlos himself—"

"Hey! Carlos! Glad you reminded me. It must be pretty near daybreak. They could be here anytime now."

It *was* pretty near daybreak. The bank clock showed 4:58 as they crossed the empty parking lot.

And, sure enough, the sidewalk outside the diner was no longer empty.

Karen was there, looking up and down the street impatiently.

"Hi, Karen!"

"Oh—good! I thought maybe you'd decided to wait someplace else."

"No," said Joe. "So what's the news? And where's Carlos? Gone looking for us?"

"Some of the news," said Karen, with a slight strained smile, "is good. We followed them. We stole a ride on their car. We found out exactly where they live. And . . ."

"And you had to walk back?"

"Quite a bit of the way, yes."

"So where's Carlos?" said Joe, still looking pleased, but beginning to glance around anxiously.

Karen's head slumped. She was chewing at her lower lip and staring down at her sneakers.

"That's the bad news."

"Eh? What? Where is he?"

"Well—not exactly bad—nothing serious—but—"

"Let me be the judge of that, Karen. Where is he?"

"He fell asleep," said Karen, still looking at her sneakers.

"*Asleep?*"

If Joe hadn't been a ghost, the whole neighborhood would have been awakened by his yell.

Then, obviously struggling to take a grip on himself, he said, in a low pleading voice: "Where, Karen—*where?*"

"Just on the edge of town. That's why it isn't so bad. I mean, he could have fallen asleep miles from here."

Joe still looked worried.

"It isn't so bad if it's a Minor Sleep—no," he said. "But what if it turns out to be a *Major* Sleep?"

Karen looked up sharply. Her eyes widened with alarm.

Danny groaned.

"Oh, *no!*"

Newcomer though he was to the world of ghosts, even he knew how bad it would be if Carlos had fallen into *that* kind of sleep!

11
"Welcome Aboard!"

In the few months that he'd been a ghost, Danny had realized that ghosts didn't get tired the normal way. They didn't really get tired at all—anymore than they got hungry or thirsty.

But, as with food and drink, the ghost's old lifetime habits tended to cling. So, just as they sometimes *thought* they were hungry or thirsty, they also imagined from time to time that they were sleepy.

When that happened—and there was nothing important to do—a ghost would find a quiet spot, sit or lie down, and close his eyes. Then he'd allow his thoughts to wander and drift. Maybe he'd think about when he was alive. Maybe he'd think about his strange new existence. Maybe he'd think about the other ghosts and what he'd learned from them. And so on.

But at those times he would never lose consciousness. Other ghosts, happening to come across him like
that—stretched out, with his eyes closed—would say:
"Hush! Danny's having a quiet think." Or: "Danny's
still not used to this existence. He still has the sleeping
habit." Or: "Danny's having a simulated sleep."

One thing no ghost would ever say is: "There's
Danny Green. Fast asleep!"

The reason for that was a very curious one.

Ghosts did in fact run out of energy. Without feeling the least bit tired, they would suddenly go out like
lights. It could happen anywhere, any time. They
could be talking to other ghosts. They could be
watching their living relatives with keen interest.
They could be making an important journey. They
could simply be crossing a street. But when their energy got below a certain level—*wham!*—they would
drop off instantly.

This happened about once a month. A ghost would
suddenly lose consciousness for anywhere up to
twenty-four hours. During that time he wouldn't
dream. He wouldn't know a thing about it. But when
he woke up—on the exact spot where he'd fallen
asleep—he would be instantly fully conscious again,
recharged with a fresh supply of energy.

Joe called this a Minor Sleep.

"If that was a Minor Sleep," Danny had asked then,
"what's a *Major* Sleep?"

"That's something else again!" said Joe. "That happens only about once a year, thank goodness! That's

like a major overhaul—it lasts for days. Sometimes more than a week."

And the reason a ghost would never say, "Look! There's one of our guys having a Major or Minor Sleep!" was this: *Whenever a ghost dropped off like that, he became invisible. Instantly. Even to other ghosts.*

"Nobody knows exactly what happens," Joe had said. "Nobody knows whether the recharging is done on the spot, or whether we're spirited away someplace else and then brought back. All I can tell you is that you wake up just where you fell asleep. Hours later, if it's a Minor Sleep. *Days* later, if it's a Major Sleep. Which," Joe added gravely, "can be a big nuisance."

Well, thought Danny, that Wednesday morning, it sure is a nuisance now!

The others were thinking the same.

"I mean if Carlos has been taken out for a Major Sleep, we might never be able to contact Wacko until after Friday's break-in!" said Joe.

"Yes," said Karen. "And even if it's a Minor Sleep he could be too late to keep that appointment with Buzz Phillips this afternoon."

"Oh, *no!*" groaned Danny. "Hey—what time did it happen, Karen?"

"About fifteen minutes before you met me."

"Which would make it about—uh—four-forty," murmured Joe. "Which means it could even be tomorrow morning before he wakes up."

"My last Minor Sleep was only *ten* hours," said Karen, hopefully.

"Yeah—but the way Carlos has been using up his energy lately—" Joe broke off. "Had there been a lot of mental work to do, following the route taken by those guys?"

"Some. It wasn't too bad at first. About eight miles south on 246. Then, just before we reached Millton Depot, they took a right, up into the hills. It got a bit tricky then."

"So where do they live—Roscoe and Kelly? A farm? Summer cabin?"

"No. They have one of those small camper trailers, tucked away on an old logging trail. But don't worry about that. *I* could give a very clear description of the route and the exact location."

"I'm sure you could," said Joe. "But who to? And how? Without Carlos to work that word processor?"

Karen sighed.

"Sorry! I forgot." Then she shrugged. "We'll just have to cross our fingers and hope that it *is* a Minor Sleep, I guess."

"Yeah!" grunted Danny. "And a short one, too. I mean how's Buzz gonna take it if all Wacko can do is introduce him to a *blank screen?*"

At 3:31 that afternoon, as he followed Wacko Williams up the stairs, Buzz Phillips was frowning thoughtfully. Wacko had *seemed* serious, but....

"Uh—are you sure that was absolutely necessary?" he asked.

Wacko glanced back

"What? Waiting by the open door? Yes. *Very* necessary."

"But—well—ghosts. I mean—"

"I know. It seems strange. After reading all the traditional ghost stories, where they always walk *through* solid objects. But when you come to think of it, it makes some sort of sense. Like, say, the wind. *It* can't go through solid objects, can it? Yet you can't see the wind, either. That's insubstantial too."

"Yeah, but the wind can get through cracks."

"Exactly what I said to—uh—them," said Wacko, pausing at the open door of his room. "And the answer was that ghosts *could* do that, but only with— Anyway, why take *my* word? In a minute you'll be able to ask them yourself."

Wacko sounded so confident as he pointed Buzz to a second chair in front of the word processor that Buzz felt a shiver run down his back. Hearing Wacko *talk* about this weird experiment was one thing. Seeing him in action—being there—on the brink of joining it yourself—that was something else.

"So," Wacko was saying, "I switch on—like that—and now we're all set."

He turned from the machine and addressed the air behind Buzz's head: "OK, you guys! I've brought Buzz along, as you can see. I have the feeling he thinks I'm slightly crazy, but this is where we prove him wrong." Wacko switched his gaze to the space between himself and Buzz. "Ready, Carlos?"

Then he stared at the screen.

The screen remained blank.

"Carlos?"

Buzz began to grow uneasy as he noticed the tension increase in Wacko's back and shoulders.

"Carlos! Come in if you can hear me!"

Wacko was crouching forward, his eyes bulging.

Buzz coughed quietly.

"Uh—maybe it isn't switched on right. . . ."

"It is! It *is* switched on! . . . Carlos—if you're playing a trick, cut it out! Right now!"

But the screen remained blank.

At 3:58, Wacko got up from the chair. He'd spent the last twenty-five minutes explaining to Buzz more about the work he and Carlos had been doing on the word processor while Carlos was alive. He also told him more about the breakthrough and about the other ghosts and some of the exchanges he'd had with them already.

"They're late, that's all," he kept saying. "They'll be along soon, you'll see."

"Sure!" Buzz kept murmuring. "Sure, Wacko! Sure!"

But those murmurs were becoming more and more soothing, so that in the end Wacko said straight out: "Look! I know what you're thinking. But I am *not* crazy. And I am *not* sick. And I am certainly *not* fooling!"

That's when he got up.

"Ordinarily," he said, "I wouldn't check on the

door again until four-thirty. That's the arrangement we have. But this is special and I'm sure *they'll* realize that, too. Wait here, Buzz."

Buzz felt more uneasy than ever, left alone in that room with only the faintly glowing screen for company. He listened very carefully, trying to track Wacko's progress down the stairs. When he heard the distant click of the front-door screen and imagined Wacko standing there—welcoming *Invisible Beings*, for Pete's sake!—Buzz shook his head.

Wacko *had* to be sick.

He'd been working too hard on all this complicated electronics stuff.

And he, Buzz, was a fool ever to have listened to him. If it hadn't been for the mention of Danny Green, probably he never would have, either.

I mean—he thought, shivering again—suppose Wacko goes really crazy. Violent crazy. What then? He's only skinny, but crazy people can get a lot of extra strength just through being crazy. And—

"Oh, no!" he murmured aloud.

For Wacko was coming back up the stairs *talking* to them! In a low voice, sure—but not to his mother or one of his brothers—oh no! To *them!* Like they were regular human visitors!

"I suddenly thought maybe you guys might have been held up only a few minutes. So instead of waiting the full hour—"

A slight noise made Buzz turn back to the screen. Then he stood up so fast he overturned his chair.

Without anyone touching the keys, without the keys even moving, a message was flickering there!

This message:

"*Hi, Buzz! The Ghost Squad is now back in business. Welcome aboard!*"

12
Buzz Breaks New Ground

Impossible!

That was Buzz's first thought. Totally—but *totally* impossible!

When Wacko had told him about the Ghost Squad and its method of communicating, Buzz had been very doubtful, to say the least. But now, when he saw what seemed like proof of Wacko's story flickering at him on the screen, his doubt turned into sheer disbelief.

And when Wacko reached the doorway, Buzz looked hard at the other boy's hands. This had to be operated by some remote-control device, he was thinking. That was how Wacko must be getting messages onto that screen without touching the keyboard.

But Wacko's hands were empty.

He grinned when he looked at the screen.

"So you beat me up the stairs, Carlos!" he said, like he was talking to the word processor itself. "Where've you been?"

"Aw, come off it, Wacko!" said Buzz, stooping to pick up the chair. He suddenly noticed his hands were trembling. "How did you do it?"

"Huh?"

"This trick. I mean, look, I'm not mad at you or anything. But—"

"This is no trick!" said Wacko, indignantly. "*You* look!"

A new message was appearing.

"*Seems like Buzz is still very skeptical, Wacko. We suggest he talks to Danny.*"

"You see?" said Wacko, holding his hands up, open, palms outward. "I'm not doing a *thing!*"

But Buzz was still staring at the screen, where further suggestions were appearing.

"*Please leave your own chair vacant, Wacko, and turn it to one side. Danny Green is going to sit there. Buzz, please address any further questions to Danny. You cannot see him, but he's now sitting in Wacko's chair, facing you.*"

Buzz gaped at the vacant chair—then shook his head fiercely, like he was trying to rouse himself from sleep.

The screen went blank, then a single word appeared, causing Buzz to turn his head.

"*Proceed.*"

"Go on, Buzz," said Wacko. "Talk to him. Ask him something. He can hear you. His replies will show up on the screen."

"This—this is crazy!" whispered Buzz.

"You didn't think it was crazy when we worked together on exploring my dreams!" the screen replied.

"Uh—but—hey, Wacko!" Buzz turned to the other boy—the only other boy he could see. "Knock it off, huh? Danny was my friend. He's dead. You can't make jokes about—"

"I still am your friend!" said the screen. *"Buzz! Please! This is for real. Ask me something, anything, so long as it's about something nobody else could know. OK? Then I'll prove it's me."*

Buzz frowned. There was something about the way this machine was talking that really did remind him of Danny. The slightly stumbling, pleading way he had when he was trying to get a point across.

He glanced at Wacko. If this was a trick, it was not only *scientifically* clever—it was also clever in its use of words. And that was something Wacko had never really shone at, as far as Buzz knew.

He cleared his throat. He turned to the empty chair.

"OK—uh—Danny. Tell me: Who was the last living person you saw, not counting me, before—uh—the accident?"

He turned to the screen.

Nobody—but nobody—would know about that. Nobody except Danny, that was.

Then he gasped.

"Miss Gilbert, the geography teacher," the answer was appearing. *"She was driving past that afternoon, outside the old factory. Just before we went in to explore."*

Buzz blinked. He was trying to remember. *Could* anyone else have known that, after all? Was Miss Gilbert ever called as a witness at the inquest? Maybe after he, Buzz, had passed out?

"OK, OK," he said. "That's true enough." Then his eyes lit up as he thought of something that he'd only just recalled. It hadn't even been mentioned at the inquest. There was no reason it should have been. "So tell me this—uh—Danny: What was the last living *creature* you saw?"

Again the answer came swiftly and surely.

"A crow. It had been perched on a fallen beam. It had gotten hold of an old plastic dish, like the kind you get at a deli for chicken liver and stuff. There was some goo in it. And I reminded you how something like that had been in one of my dreams."

Buzz's eyes were blurred now as he turned to the vacant chair.

"Gee, Danny!" he whispered, fully convinced. "It's great to—huh!" He broke off with a small choked laugh. "I was going to say it's great to *see* you again! But you know what I mean."

"I sure do!" said Danny, via Carlos and the screen.

It really did feel like old times, Danny was thinking. The only thing different was that this way Buzz would never see the expression on *his* face. Which maybe was a good thing, Danny thought, brushing the tears from his eyes.

Joe patted him on the shoulder.

"Nice work, Danny. Only maybe we'd better get on with the main business."

Wacko seemed to be thinking the same. Almost as if he were mirroring Joe's movements and thoughts, he gave Buzz a pat on *his* shoulder and said to the space in front of the word processor: "So what held you up, Carlos?"

"*I fell asleep,*" came the reply.

There was a pause. Carlos had turned to Joe.

"Do I tell them about our special way of sleeping?"

"Why not?"

"Looks like you'll have to anyway," said Karen, smiling and nodding toward Wacko, who was looking annoyed.

"So how come the others didn't wake you in time?" he asked. "Buzz and I were wondering what had gone wrong. I mean it's *important*, you guys—keeping appointments promptly. I mean—"

Buzz had touched him on the arm and was pointing to the screen, which suddenly seemed to explode with words.

"*All right, all right, all right! Think we don't know that ourselves? So cool it, OK? Just sit, go on—sit down, and I'll tell you how I went to sleep, and why I slept for ten hours, and why we're lucky it was only ten hours, and why nobody and nothing, ghost, man, woman, boy, girl, nothing in this whole world could*" *ever have woken me up one lousy second earlier. . . ."*

Then the two boys stared, while Carlos explained all about the different kinds of ghost sleep.

Buzz was fascinated. And, being a complete newcomer to the whole idea, he wasn't slow to respond when Carlos wound up his essay on ghost sleep with an abrupt: *"Any questions?"*

"Yes!"

And for the next half hour or so, the complete Ghost Squad, plus Wacko, worked hard answering Buzz's keen, intelligent queries about what they could and could not do. And why they came back as ghosts anyway. And what happened about food and drink. And did they feel the heat and cold. And dozens more.

Some of the answers were already known to Wacko, but there was something about the way Buzz probed that seemed to make the total picture clearer, so that even the Ghost Squad members began to feel better for Buzz's questioning. It seemed to help them make more complete contact with the living. And when the subject turned to what ghosts could do to make their presence felt *without* the word processor, Buzz showed how really valuable his help could be.

Joe had been explaining, through Carlos, just what could be done with finely balanced objects. Then Danny had joined in to remind Joe of the effect of touch—the faint sensation a living person experienced whenever a ghost touched him or her.

"You mean you *can* make yourselves felt?" Buzz asked, when Joe had mentioned this fact. "You *can* make living persons feel you?"

"Yes, but only very faintly. Usually so faintly that the person isn't even aware of it."

"Well—hey!—but this is important!" said Buzz, sitting back and looking around rapidly. "Look—one of you touch *me*. You do it, Danny. Go on. Only don't tell me where."

Grinning sheepishly, Danny grabbed his old friend's left ear and gave it a sharp twist.

Immediately, Buzz put a hand up to that ear.

"There! Right? My left ear. Like a slight draft. No—more like a small drop of cold water. Or no—a fly—a fly just brushing it."

"*Correct!*" said the screen.

"OK. Now someplace else. Go on. . . . My *right* ear? . . . Good! . . . My nose? . . . Well OK, my top lip just *under* my nose. That's what I meant anyway. . . ."

So the strange test continued, with Buzz scoring nine out of ten—or even better, allowing for the nose/lip mix-up.

Then Buzz asked for a similar set of tests to be run on Wacko, and the results were just as accurate.

"So don't you see what this means?" Buzz asked, his eyes shining. "It means," he went on, without waiting for an answer, "that what happened earlier—you being late—Carlos not being available—Wacko getting worried—could have been made less of a problem. I mean at least you could have touched us, to show that some of you were around, even if Carlos couldn't make it."

"Hey—wow—that *would* have helped!" said Wacko, looking pleased.

But he didn't look half so pleased as Danny when Buzz then went on to say: "In fact this way we have a really good backup system available. A standby in case the word processor breaks down, or Carlos goes to sleep again, or we're operating away from this house, in the streets, say. Anyplace we don't have access to the machine here."

"But—"

"Come on, Wacko! Just think what we can do if it's understood that a touch on the right ear means just that: *Right! Yes! Affirmative!* And a touch on the left ear mean *No.* Get the picture, you guys?"

His invisible listeners were so delighted that four invisible hands reached to touch him on the right ear.

Danny even gave *Wacko's* right ear a tug for good measure, as Joe said: "Given the right questions we can get a whole lot of information across just by answering yes or no."

"I told you Buzz would be a real help, didn't I? Huh? Didn't I? Didn't I tell you?"

Grinning, Joe grabbed and pulled at Danny's right ear. And that *didn't* feel like a drop of rain or a fly! Then: "OK, OK!" he said. "Simmer down, you guys. So now we have a terrifically useful new technique at our—uh—fingertips. And a terrifically useful new member on the team. But we still have a job to do. So, Carlos, let's get busy with the briefing. First, the latest details about Roscoe and Kelly; then the dope on Chester Adams. With a bit of luck, we can now clear up both cases tomorrow...."

13
Chester Backs Off

The following morning, after getting off the school bus, Wacko Williams went through a rerun of what he had done two days earlier.

At least it started out as a rerun.

Buzz Phillips had wanted to be with him when he tackled Chester Adams this time, but Wacko refused.

"No, thanks, Buzz. If I can't handle him with the information I now have, I *deserve* to get dumped in a garbage can!"

So Buzz watched from a distance as Wacko waited by the school gate, once again pretending to be leafing through a book.

And once again Wacko didn't have long to wait.

"Chester Adams."

The bully looked up at the quiet greeting. When he saw who it was, a frown crossed his face—to be quickly replaced by a sneer.

"Well, well, *well!* If it isn't Wacko Williams! Hi, *Wacko!* You don't mind me calling you *Wacko*, do you?"

"I'd prefer Henry, from *you*," said Wacko. "But suit yourself."

"You bet I'll suit myself, *Wacko*. . . . So what do you want this time? Another little chat around the corner? Just between us and the garbage cans, Heh! heh!"

"As a matter of fact, yes," said Wacko quietly. "And when you hear what I've got to say, I think you'll prefer it that way, too."

The grin wobbled a little on Chester's face. There was something so strangely confident in Wacko's manner.

"OK," he said cautiously. "You lead the way."

When it became apparent that they would be alone again around the corner, Chester's sneer returned.

"You sure are a glutton for punishment, Wacko! Or have you decided to pick another subject this time? Something that won't get me mad at you?"

"Yes. It is another subject, in a way," said Wacko, taking his stance in exactly the same place, right in front of one of the cans.

"Only 'in a way'? You'd better be careful, Wacko. You know what happened on Tuesday!"

"I certainly do," said Wacko. "Tuesday night as well as Tuesday morning."

Chester shrugged.

"I was talking about Tuesday morning. Right here."

"Yes," said Wacko, with a smile, "but I prefer to talk about Tuesday *night*."

Chester looked puzzled.

"What about Tuesday night?"

"I wanted to ask you something about it, if I may."

"Sure you may. But if I don't like what it is, you know what to expect. Like if it's about whether I got on to those Green kids about their thieving ways again. Is it?"

"Oh no, Chester, no! It isn't about *their* thieving ways. No. All I want to ask you is *this*." Wacko wasn't smiling now. He looked straight into those little eyes and said, *"Did Theodore enjoy his supper?"*

If Chester had been standing with *his* back to the garbage cans, he probably would have ended up the way Wacko had. It was like *he'd* been shoved back with a powerful thrust.

"What—? Who—? How—?"

With each broken question he took a step back. His face had flushed crimson and his eyes no longer looked small, they'd popped so wide.

"What do I mean?" said Wacko, still fixing him steadily with that cool penetrating stare. "I mean did Theodore enjoy that twenty-dollar bill you fed him! *That's* what I mean!"

Chester was speechless. All he could do was gape. At the mention of the twenty-dollar bill, his hands had begun to shake so hard that he dropped one of his books. He didn't even seem to notice it.

"Well," said Wacko, "why don't you answer me? I asked politely enough, didn't I?"

"But—but—hey, Wacko! How—?"

"The name is Henry. To *you*, Chessy-wess!"

"Yeah—sorry, Henry! But—hey—that name! And—and—" Chester gulped and shook his head. Then hoarsely he started again: "But *nobody* knows about—"

Again he broke off. His eyes had narrowed once more, but in puzzlement.

"Nobody knows about the teddy bear?" said Wacko, helpfully. "Well, I wouldn't say that. There's you, and your folks—"

"But they wouldn't tell anybody!"

"—and now there's me. *I* know about Theodore. But I bet your folks don't know about his peculiar eating habits, do they, Chessy-wess? Even though the—uh—food comes out of their cash register."

Chester looked around anxiously.

"Hey, Wack— I mean Henry— I don't know how you know about this, but please—"

"That's OK, Chester. I won't snitch on you. So long as you put that money back where you found it. Including the bills you'd already stashed inside Theodore. And do it soon!"

"I will, Henry, promise! As soon as I get home!"

"You'd better! Because I'll find out if you don't keep that promise. I'll know. You won't be able to hide it from me. OK?"

"OK! Sure! Sure, Henry! But—hey—" Chester was

aiming for a friendly smile, but it came out very crooked. "Is this—was this—some kind of scientific thing? Huh? One of your inventions? Something to see through walls with? I mean—*right through into my room!* Wow!"

"Let's just say I have friends who look out for me," said Wacko softly. "Let's just say they'll be checking on you from now on, and that you'd better quit your thieving ways."

"Sure! I—it was really only a joke—but—"

"And also stop accusing other people of being thieves when you don't really know the truth!"

"You mean—?"

"I mean Mike and Jilly Green, yes. I *especially* mean Mike and Jilly Green. Because if my friends— and I'm talking about *invisible* friends now—ever see you bugging those kids again, you'd better plan on getting right out of town. Shutting yourself in your room certainly won't help you, will it?"

Chester opened his mouth, but again words failed him.

"Is all that clear—Chester?"

"Uh—yes—sure, Henry," came the whispered reply.

"All right. Now beat it. You're beginning to annoy me."

After Chester had scurried off around the corner, Wacko allowed his face muscles to relax. Buzz had started out to see if anything was wrong, but by the time he reached Wacko, the answer was obvious. The grin that was now lighting up Wacko's face said it all.

"I take it that Case Number One has been thoroughly cleared up!" said Buzz, grinning back.

"You bet! I only hope we take care of the Roscoe-Kelly business just as successfully." Wacko paused. He glanced around. "Right, guys?"

His hunch was correct.

What felt like four flies brushed his right ear in quick succession.

14
The Clearing in the Woods

There was no need to rely on hunches when Buzz and Wacko went into action on the second case, that afternoon. It had been agreed that the Ghost Squad would definitely go with them to the police.

That was why both boys were very conscious of their ears when they sat in Detective Grogan's office.

Detective Eugene Grogan was a big man with thin sandy hair, a beaky nose and a wide unsmiling mouth.

"Now let's get this straight," he said. "You say you have information that the Hyman jewelry store is going to be broken into on Friday night?"

This was what they had told the desk sergeant. They both nodded their heads firmly.

"Right!" said Wacko.

"You even have their names? Uh—" Detective Grogan lifted a large red hand and uncovered the scrap of paper the sergeant had given him. "Roscoe and Kelly? That correct?"

"Yes, sir," said Wacko.

"And their descriptions?" The detective lifted his hand again. "Both in late teens or early twenties? Roscoe short, with blond hair? Kelly taller, heavier, with dark beard?"

"Uh—yes, sir." Wacko sounded less confident. "That was our information. We haven't seen them ourselves."

Detective Grogan grunted.

"And they drive an old black Plymouth, license-plate number unknown?"

"Yes," said Wacko. "I guess it was all caked up with mud and—well. . . ."

He stopped himself from adding that although their informants had had *time* to wipe it clean, they just didn't have the ability.

"But the rest of our information was very reliable, sir!" said Buzz.

Grogan gave him a sour look.

"Yet the sergeant tells me you're not prepared to reveal your source. That right?"

He was still looking at Buzz. Buzz wondered if the detective was remembering that he'd had dealings with him before. Once, when Danny was alive and had predicted a robbery at the school. It had taken Grogan quite a time to get rid of his suspicion that *they* had had something to do with it. An understandable suspicion, true—but it hadn't been pleasant for either Buzz or Danny.

"We promised not to say who'd told us," Buzz said, knowing well enough how Grogan would take it if they *did* tell him. "But it really is reliable information, sir."

Still Detective Grogan gave no spoken hint that he remembered Buzz. But the look in those sandy-lashed eyes was cold and unfriendly.

At last he turned to Wacko.

"Have you told your father about this?"

His tone was still quite cool, but there was a more respectful look in his eyes.

Buzz sighed. Last time, it was Danny who'd been given the rougher treatment. Because of his poor home background. This time it looked like he, Buzz, would be the one out of favor. Because of Wacko's *special* home background.

Detective Grogan must certainly have recognized *him*. The question about Wacko's father proved it. Mr. Williams was a lawyer. Not only that, he was a valued member of the State's Attorney's department.

"No, sir," said Wacko. "It was part of our promise. We were told to give the information to the police and no one else."

The sandy lashes flickered.

"I see. And you say you know where Roscoe and Kelly are living. In a trailer, right? Over toward Millton Depot?"

"Correct, sir."

Detective Grogan frowned.

"Yes, well, before I call the Millton sheriff's department and ask them to run a check on those two guys, I need the precise location. A trailer in a clearing in the woods isn't enough. Can you be more specific? . . . *No?*"

The boys were shaking their heads even before they felt the brushing on their left ears.

They had talked this over with the Ghost Squad. It had been decided that, rather than risk the detective having to rely on second-hand verbal directions, Buzz and Wacko should go along with him. With Karen and Carlos as stowaways.

Joe had explained why.

"Then if there's any doubt about which turning to take, you can use the Ear Code."

Grogan's frown had deepened.

"Well?"

"No, sir," said Wacko. "It—it's sort of complicated. But if we went along there with you, we could show you. I mean *exactly.*"

Detective Grogan was staring hard at them. But they both looked totally serious.

"OK," he said, glancing at his watch. "We'll go there now. But remember—" He lifted a warning finger. "You stay in the car at all times. I shall probably not challenge these men, even if they happen to be home. It isn't on my territory, and I wouldn't be allowed to question them merely on suspicion anyway."

"No, sir," said Wacko. "I understand."

"So I'll be simply pretending to be a motorist who's lost his way. *But*"—here Detective Grogan looked very fierce—"you never know. They might get suspicious. Then things could get rough. So—"

"We'll stay in the car, sir. Don't worry!"

The car ride was the strangest either Buzz or Wacko had ever been on.

It was straightforward enough most of the way. For the first eight miles along Route 246 they had no need to fall back on the Ear Code. But over every yard of those eight miles both Buzz and Wacko were conscious of the plan laid down by Joe Armstrong: *"Try and get in the back seat together. . . ."*

Well, that hadn't been difficult. Grogan had ordered them to sit there, in fact.

"Carlos will sit between you. Karen up front. Karen and Carlos will consult with each other if there's any doubt about the correct route. Should you overshoot a right turn, Carlos will give Wacko two quick tugs on the right ear. If you overshoot a left turn, he'll give Buzz two on the left ear. Got it?"

"Yes," Buzz had replied. "But what about the routine yes/no part of the code?"

"Those will be single touches, as usual. But only in reply to your spoken questions. OK?"

And so they sat—tense, alert for signals, and as far apart as possible.

And when they finally left Route 246 and started climbing into the wooded hills, it became stranger than ever.

"Where now?"

"Straight ahead. Right, Carl—uh—Buzz?"

Buzz hesitated. Then he felt the single brush on his right ear and sighed with relief.

"Yes!"

The narrow country road began to twist and turn. Not only that, but it seemed like the whole hillside was a network of minor roads. As they passed yet another branch or intersection the boys would close their eyes, waiting for the two tugs that would tell them they'd gone too far.

When they came to a burned-out roadside cabin that they'd been told was a landmark for the logging trail, next on the left, they nearly fouled up.

"Hey!" said Buzz. "Was that—?"

Carlos, in his excitement, gave him no fewer than *four* quick tugs. But on the *right* ear!

"What's *that* supposed to mean?" Buzz couldn't help yelling.

Grogan slowed down.

"What's going on back there?"

"Nothing! I mean—I think we should be looking for the trail somewhere on the left, sir."

"Yes," said Wacko, guessing what had been going on between his excitable friend, the late Carlos Gomez, and Buzz. "In fact—just here—see it?"

He was glad to feel a single, very unmistakable brushing against his right ear.

"Huh!" grunted Grogan, making the turn. "Cut out the fooling. This is a serious matter. *If* your information is reliable!"

There was no further misunderstanding. The dirt trail wound through the woods for about eight-tenths of a mile before petering out in a clearing. The clearing was partly screened by a pile of rotting logs, long since abandoned to the weeds.

"*And in that clearing, behind those logs, you will find the trailer,*" had been the final instructions on the word processor.

Well, the logs were there. The weeds were there. The clearing was there.

But even before Grogan had finally stopped the car, it was plain to everyone present—man, boys and ghosts—that there just wasn't any trailer there!

"Are you *sure* this is the place?"

Detective Grogan looked sourer than ever. Sour, suspicious, snappish.

Buzz and Wacko looked at each other. They were both thinking the same thing. Were *Karen and Carlos* sure?

Without waiting for a sign from the ghosts, Buzz decided to chance a positive reply.

"Well, yes, sir! After all, we followed the route as described to us. And it did lead to a clearing. And—and—well—trailers *are* mobile. They must have moved on."

The detective gave him a last lingering stare. Then he sighed and got out of the car.

"You stay here. I'll take a look around."

As soon as he was out of earshot, bending and peering at the ground, Buzz glared at the space between himself and Wacko.

"*Are* you two guys sure this is the place?" he asked, fiercely.

"Of *course* we're sure, you dummy, and if you don't believe us, get out and take a look over there, at the far side there, in the undergrowth, where we saw them dumping empty cans and other garbage, go on, take a look!"

"Carlos!" said Karen, looking at her fellow ghost bouncing up and down on the back seat, seething with annoyance. "They can't hear you! Remember? Just tell him yes or no."

"What d'ya mean—yes or no? The answer's yes! Of course this is the place! *I'm* sure even if you aren't!"

"All right! So simmer down. *I'm* sure, too."

"So—yes!" said Carlos, giving Buzz a belt on the right ear that would have deafened him in normal circumstances. "And—yes!" he added, reaching out and giving Wacko's right ear a savage tug.

"It took you long enough to decide!" said Wacko accusingly, giving that ear a flick.

"Oh, if only we'd developed a portable word processor!" groaned Carlos. "Battery operated! . . . The cans! The garbage! You can see the place from here! Look at the bugs!"

Sure enough, over the spot where the hoods had dumped their garbage, there was a small cloud of flies.

"I wonder—" murmured Karen.

"What?"

"Something Joe's pretty good at. I wonder if I could do it."

She eased herself through the open window at the

driver's side. Carlos watched her as she ran across the clearing behind the stooping figure of Grogan.

"Hey! What are you going to do?" he called out.

"You'll see," she said, walking into the brush to where the flies still danced and hovered. "I hope!"

"Oh, *that!*" said Carlos, as she stood there, eyes shut, frowning with concentration. "I doubt if . . . uh . . . well, maybe . . . it's worth a—*wow!*"

Karen proved to be better at the task than she'd dared hope.

Buzz, who'd been telling Wacko in a low voice about his previous brush with Grogan, broke off.

"Hey! Wacko! Look at those flies!"

They had now closed up as if an invisible net had been drawn over them. *A net in the shape of a headless human body!*

Wacko stared.

"I wonder—hey!—what if it's Carlos? Trying to tell us something?"

A brush against his left ear told him he was wrong. "Is it Karen?"

This time his right ear received the signal.

Wacko grabbed Buzz's arm.

"It *is!*" he said. "It's Karen. She must want us to go over there. Let's—*uh-oh!*"

Detective Grogan had just straightened up. He must have caught the movement of the flies out of the corner of his eye. He turned swiftly, half crouching.

The cloud of flies suddenly expanded, loosened and lost its shape as the man strode toward them. By the time he'd reached the spot, they were buzzing angrily at this double disturbance: the sudden removal of the ghostly net and the approach of the man. The detective stood looking down at the garbage. Karen returned to the car.

"Not bad!" said Carlos. "You had *me* feeling spooked for a minute there!"

"I just can't bear them near my face, though!" said Karen. "Even though I know they can't bite me."

"Anyway, it worked. *Now* maybe he'll believe Buzz and Wacko."

"Did you find something over there, sir?" Buzz asked, when the detective returned, still brushing away a few lingering flies.

"Yeah!" grunted the man. "Garbage. Cans, food containers, stuff like that."

"Well, that proves those guys were here then, doesn't it?" said Wacko.

"It proves *someone* was here. That's all. It could be a regular picnic spot, or a teenage hangout."

And that was all he would say.

The journey back was made in silence—anxious and uneasy in the passenger seats; thoughtful, brooding and increasingly distrustful in the driver's.

15
Joe's Master Plan

The complete Ghost Squad met again that evening in Wacko's room. It was a tense, urgent meeting. With only twenty-four hours to go before the break-in was due, there were two big questions on their minds:

1. Had Roscoe and Kelly abandoned their plan and left the area?
2. Was Detective Grogan taking the warning seriously?

In connection with #1, Joe and Danny had been patrolling the town all the time the others were taking the car ride, and they'd seen no sign of the two hoods.

"But that doesn't necessarily mean they've given up

on the job," Joe pointed out, via Carlos and the word processor. "*They could be resting up, lying low. And maybe they've moved the trailer to a better place.*"

Buzz was more concerned with Question #2.

"I didn't like the way Grogan got so quiet and thoughtful."

"Me either," said Wacko.

"Every time I looked up at the rearview mirror, there were his eyes. Looking at *me!* Very, very suspiciously."

"So what happens if these guys do hit the Hyman place and Grogan doesn't show?" said Wacko.

"That's what I've been thinking," said Danny to the other ghosts.

"Yeah, but maybe Buzz has it all wrong," said Carlos. "Maybe the detective got so quiet because he was planning a stakeout."

"I agree," said Karen. "Detectives don't go around discussing their next moves with civilians. Even civilians who've given them helpful information."

Joe smiled grimly.

"As a victim myself, whose murder hasn't even been *suspected* by the police, let alone solved by them, I don't share your great faith in detectives. But from now on until our next full meeting, you two will get your chance to prove that Grogan *is* on the ball."

"Oh?"

"How?"

"You'll be following him around. Seeing what inquiries he makes connected with Roscoe and Kelly.

What other neighboring police departments and agencies he contacts. And like that."

Carlos and Karen looked pleased.

"What about me?" said Danny.

"You stick with me," said Joe. "We continue to look out for Roscoe and Kelly. Only this time we'll take into account something new."

"Like what?"

"Like maybe they've changed their appearance."

"*Disguised* themselves?"

"Sort of. Even if Roscoe's only dyed his hair, or Kelly's shaved his beard off."

"Hey! Are you guys still there?" said Wacko.

"*Affirmative!*" said the word processor.

"So what about Grogan?" said Buzz.

"*Don't worry!*" came the reply. "*We're looking into that. By tomorrow afternoon at three-thirty, we should have a much clearer picture. In the meantime, keep calm and get plenty of rest. Tomorrow looks like our big day.*"

But when 3:30 the following afternoon came around, there was still great doubt. Heavy clouds had been gathering outside for the past five or six hours, and heavy clouds hung over the Ghost Squad as it made its report.

"*No sign of Roscoe and Kelly as yet,*" Joe relayed through Carlos. "*But don't let that get you down. It's quite usual for burglars to keep clear of the target premises on the day of the break-in.*"

"That figures," said Buzz. His face was looking pale and strained. Danny guessed he hadn't had much sleep the night before. "So what about Detective Grogan? *Is* he taking this seriously?"

The word processor seemed to give Carlos some difficulty.

"Well yes and no—" it began.

Then it was erased.

"We took every opportunity—"

Then that was erased.

"He's a very quiet man. I mean he doesn't say much to anybody about anything, so—"

And that too was erased.

Then the bad news was released.

"The only call we heard him make in connection with the case was to Wacko's father."

"WHAT?!" cried Wacko.

"The call was aborted, however, when he was told that Mr. Williams is presently in Washington."

"That's true!" said Wacko, with a sigh of relief. "But—uh—why? Why should he—?"

"*I* know why!" said Buzz. "It's what I've been afraid of. It means he's definitely remembered about Danny and me."

"You mean he thinks we've been playing a trick on him?"

"No. Not that bad. But if it's like the other time, he probably thinks we're kidding *ourselves.* That it's another psychic experiment."

"Well so it is! Except it's no experiment. It's a fact."

"Yeah! But try telling *Grogan* that! Anyway, he

probably wanted to warn your father about the company you're keeping. Telling him I'm some kind of nut who's having a bad influence on his son. I mean it won't help when he points out that my last partner in foretelling the future is—uh—dead."

Buzz looked around.

"I'm sorry, Danny, but that's the way *he'll* think of you."

Wacko nodded thoughtfully.

"It seems to me that Roscoe and Kelly had *better* make their move tonight! It's the only way Grogan will ever believe we haven't been fooling around."

The ghosts had been listening in worried silence. Danny especially was beginning to feel the same kind of despair as Buzz's.

Then Joe forced a grin, clapped his hands and said: "Carlos, before this turns into a regular wake, transmit the following message. . . ."

The word processor went into action.

"Anyway, assuming Roscoe and Kelly do make their move tonight—and also assuming that Grogan does sit on his hands—here's what we *do. . . ."*

There was a pause. Then: *"One: We'll undertake the stakeout of the Hyman store ourselves.*

"Two: As soon as Roscoe and Kelly are seen to be breaking in, we'll call the police. They'll have to act then!

"Three—"

"Hold it!" Buzz was shaking his head vigorously. "You're getting it all wrong, you guys. *We* can't stay out half the night. Our folks would never allow it, and we might not be able to sneak out unnoticed. So—"

"*So no one was going to suggest you did!*" said the word processor.

"So all right! So if there's only going to be you ghosts staking out, how are you going to make a phone call?"

"Right!" said Wacko. "I mean unless Carlos has mastered some technique . . ." He broke off. "Hey—*have* you, Carlos?"

"*No, dummy! But what Joe is trying to tell you, if you'll just shut up, is this. You are going to be making the calls. You and Buzz. Even though you will not be at the stakeout. Even though you'll be home, in the comfort of your rooms.*"

Buzz and Wacko looked at each other.

Could ghosts suddenly go crazy, just like living people?

"Yes, but *how?*"

"Yeah! *How?*"

"*Listen!*" came the reply. "*Pay close attention. . . .*"

When Joe had finished unfolding his plan, Buzz and Wacko broke out in grins for the first time that day.

"Wow!" cried Wacko. "This should be terrific! Right, Buzz?"

"Right!"

Buzz looked around with shining eyes.

"Joe! I'm not sure exactly where you are, but—you're a genius!"

16
"A Possible Murder!"

The storm finally broke at about 6:30, and for a few hours it raged so fiercely that it looked like it would ruin the plans of everyone: ghosts and kids, crooks and victims. Crash after crash of thunder shook buildings for miles around. Streak after streak of lightning split the thick air, slashing through the curtains of rain. The creek overflowed, some low-lying streets were flooded, cars stalled and even the trains were brought to a standstill for a while, when lightning knocked out a transformer.

Only two of the ghosts had outdoor work to do in the first part of Joe's plan: Joe himself and Karen. Their task was to keep watch on the Hyman store from the time the Hymans left at 5:45 for their dinner engagement. But, being ghosts, Joe and Karen weren't affected physically when the rain came down in torrents.

Their clothes didn't get wet.

Their hair wasn't whipped about by the wind, or plastered over their faces.

As living people scurried for cover, Joe and Karen strolled calmly along their beat, first at the front of the store, then at the rear.

Once, as they turned the corner back into the main street, where the wind was at its strongest—strong enough to have sent ordinary people spinning around—Joe glanced at Karen and said: "What's wrong? What are you looking at me like that for?"

The girl shrugged and smiled sheepishly.

"Oh—nothing! I still can't get used to seeing another ghost looking so dry and unruffled when it's pouring like this."

Joe laughed.

"Yeah. Sometimes it spooks me, too. Makes you realize we *are* ghosts! That's why you never see many ghosts outdoors in weather like this, even though it doesn't affect them physically. But don't waste time looking at *me*. Save your eyes for Roscoe and Kelly."

"Do you think they'll come if it stays like this?"

"Well, it has to slacken off sooner or later. And maybe they'll figure on the storm giving them extra cover."

At 7:30, the storm still showed no signs of abating. By now the streets were practically deserted except for the occasional fire truck that came blaring along, sending up bow waves, and the few cars that swished by.

It was a car that attracted the ghosts' attention at 7:31.

"Look!" said Karen. "Right outside the jewelry store! Isn't that—?"

"Mr. and Mrs. Hyman's car? Yes! Let's go!"

As two figures got out of the car and scampered to the entrance to the living quarters at the side of the store, Joe and Karen hurried to join them and take a closer look.

"Well at least it's the Hymans themselves!" said Karen. "But why so soon?"

The man was fumbling for his keys. The woman huddled close beside him—already dripping wet from the few yards' dash.

"With our luck," said Mr. Hyman, "we'll get a ticket for parking outside our own store!"

"I keep telling you, Harry, it could have been worse! If the storm had been a couple of hours later, the building could have been struck when we were all having dinner. Then—well—*you* saw it. We'd have been trapped inside. Burned alive!"

Mr. Hyman grunted.

"Yeah. I guess so. And I guess it's safe enough leaving the car here for now. The cops'll have more important things on their minds while this lasts."

"So hurry up with the door! On a night like this, the safest place is in your own home!"

"Oh boy!" said Karen, as the door closed behind the

jeweler and his wife. "*Their* home won't be so safe. Not if Roscoe and Kelly show up!"

"Right! All the more reason for *us* to stay alert."

It wasn't until after ten o'clock that the storm passed over and the rain turned into a drizzle. Then a few people did begin to appear. Some were walking their dogs; others seemed more purposeful, as if they'd been sheltering from the storm and were in a hurry to get home before it had a chance to start again. Mr. Hyman came out and drove his car around to the back. But it wasn't long before he returned on foot and went inside again.

And although the storm didn't return, and the drizzle tapered off to a mere misty dampness, most people seemed to have decided to call it a night. The streets were deserted again at 11:35, when Karen glanced at the bank clock and said: "Well, it's beginning to look like Roscoe and Kelly have called it off."

Joe nodded.

"Possibly. I'm beginning to hope that they have. Now that the Hymans have gone to bed and the place is dark."

"Why's that?"

"Well, if the hoods come along now, they'll assume that the Hymans are still over in Sharonville, enjoying themselves. Right? So they'll go ahead with the break-in. On the other hand, if they'd come earlier and seen the lights, it would probably have made them think twice."

Karen shivered.

"Yes, I see what you mean! You think they'll go blundering in, wake up the Hymans and—Joe! Don't you think we'd better warn Carlos and Danny about this extra danger? I mean *they* won't know about the Hymans coming back so early, either!"

Joe frowned.

"It's too late now, I guess. I can't risk—oh-oh! Correction! It's too late now, I *know!*"

He was staring across the misty street to where a battered Plymouth had just pulled silently into the parking lot.

Roscoe and Kelly took their time. They spent about ten minutes just sitting in the car, watching the still quite light traffic go by. And even when they finally got out, they first strolled casually across to the station, as if they were waiting for someone to arrive on a late train.

When Karen and Joe caught up with them, they were staring at a timetable in the entrance. But the topic of their muttered conversation wasn't trains. Roscoe was getting impatient.

"Aw, come on, Kelly! What's with you tonight?"

"Just a precaution. You never know who might have been looking out of their window. They see us now, they think, 'Huh! Just a couple of guys waiting for a train!'"

"So—great! So what are we supposed to do? Stay here until a train gets in? Then what?"

"No. We don't wait here. We stroll away like we've found out the train's been delayed and we have half an hour to kill and we feel like stretching our legs. OK?"

Roscoe only grunted.

The men walked slowly back across the parking lot and onto the street. Kelly kept glancing at his watch, probably to keep up the pretense.

"But he's overdoing it," said Joe. "He's *talking* cool, but my guess is he's very nervous."

"Who wouldn't be, with a buddy like Roscoe?"

Both men were wearing dark shirts and jeans. When they turned the corner of the block, into a darker area of backyards, old sheds and makeshift garages, they began to merge with the shadows. But even then Kelly still walked like a human being—a rather skulking, furtive figure, yes, but still a *person*.

Roscoe was different.

As soon as he entered the shadows, his whole form seemed to change. His shoulders hunched, his arms disappeared, his feet seemed to glide rather than walk.

"Like a prowling cat!" said Karen, whispering in spite of the fact that only Joe would have been able to hear, even if she'd shouted.

"Like one of us!" murmured Joe. "Almost!"

"Huh! If *he* was a ghost, he'd be a Malev for sure!" said Karen, using the name they had for the very worst type of ghost—the sort whose reason for staying around on earth was to do as much evil as they possibly could. "Look at him now!"

Roscoe's face—hidden from Kelly in the shadows, but quite discernible to Karen and Joe—was a picture of malice and contempt.

Kelly was saying: "I don't like this. It just doesn't feel right."

Roscoe's expression became uglier. He was walking behind Kelly, and as he replied he seemed unable to prevent himself from lifting one hand in a swift clawing movement toward his companion's right cheek.

"Come *on!*" he said, in a snarly whisper. "It's nerves, is all!"

"Huh-uh! It's timing. The timing's wrong. It's late. They could be back any time now. If only we hadn't had to make that stupid detour!"

"Late nothing. They could be hours yet. Those Vet functions go on half the night. Anyways, *they* could get delayed by floods, too."

"Well, there's the backyard. The one with the white gate. You ready?"

Kelly turned.

Roscoe had stopped. He was bending over on one knee. To Karen, he looked like a cat that was just about to lick itself.

"Sure! Just checking my shoelace. You go ahead. Try the gate. They could have left it unlocked. You never know your luck."

While Roscoe muttered these words, hunched in the deepest part of the shadow, he seemed to be doing just what he'd said: tugging, testing, retying a knot.

But Joe and Karen knew better.

With their ghostly vision, they saw that he was lifting up the right leg of his jeans to check on something taped to the inside of his calf—something fairly bulky but compact, with a dark oily sheen.

"A gun!" gasped Karen.

"Which Kelly isn't supposed to know about! This is getting to look bad—real bad!"

"Shall I—"

Joe nodded.

"Yes! Nothing's going to stop that guy now. In another few minutes, they'll be over the wall and into the back of the store. So—quick as you can—alert the others and tell them to call the cops right away. With a bit of luck we'll be able to stop a successful break-in, maybe even a—"

Already Karen had vanished around the corner, on her way. And already Roscoe was giving Kelly a boost over the wall. Joe shrugged and finished what he was saying anyway.

"—maybe even a possible murder!"

17
"It All Depends on You!"

Danny Green was feeling uneasy. It was getting close to midnight, and he still hadn't heard from Joe and Karen.

Danny was standing at the window of Buzz Phillips's bedroom. He'd been in that bedroom for hours. He'd been there ever since he'd walked home with Buzz, after the meeting at Wacko's place. He'd been there while Buzz had had his supper and while Buzz had taken a shower before coming to bed.

He'd started to feel uneasy when he'd seen Buzz getting into bed and making himself comfortable, propped against the pillows. He knew that Buzz *meant* to stay awake. That was essential to the success of Joe's plan.

But Danny also knew that Buzz was very tired, and that the more comfortable he got, the more likely he was to nod off.

After all, that was how he came to get the nickname Buzz. Ever since he'd dropped off to sleep in a history class and started to snore softly: *Buzzzz . . . Buzzzz.*

Danny winced at the memory.

So long as Buzz didn't do it tonight!

He glanced across. Buzz's eyes were still open. But only just.

Suddenly, like he knew Danny was staring at him, Buzz gave his head a shake. His eyes opened wider.

"You still there, Danny?"

Danny breathed a sigh of relief. He almost ran across the softly lit room to touch Buzz's right ear.

"Good!" said Buzz. Then: "No word yet?"

Danny touched his left ear.

"Good . . ." Buzz's eyes began to glaze. He gave his head another shake. He grinned. "I bet you've been worrying, thinking I might fall asleep . . . right?"

Danny touched his right ear.

"Righ—" Buzz's eyes closed. He didn't finish the word. He gave his head another shake. "Danny? You still here?"

"Oh boy!" muttered Danny, giving Buzz's ear an extra-firm tug. "He's so sleepy he's repeating himself!"

He went back to the window. The mist was swirling slowly under the lighted porch window of the house opposite. Otherwise there was no movement in the street below.

"If nothing happens soon," he muttered, "it'll be too late. Let's hope Wacko isn't getting sleepy!"

The thought of Wacko cheered him up a little. It really had been a good plan—the sort of plan that took care of such emergencies. Danny went over it in his mind. He heard Joe's voice again as he dictated it to Carlos. He saw it written out again as Carlos transmitted it to the screen.

"*As soon as Roscoe and Kelly make their move, probably over the wall in back of the store, Karen will run to your houses, Wacko and Buzz. There's no need to have any doors open. Karen won't need to enter. Carlos will be watching out from Wacko's room window. Danny will be watching from Buzz's. Then when Karen gives the go-ahead, Carlos will touch Wacko's top lip and he'll make Call Number One to the police. Likewise Danny and Buzz a few minutes later. Buzz will make Call Number Two. That should get results!*"

Danny turned. Buzz's eyes were still open, but only in slits. Danny wondered if it would be possible to resume the conversation they'd had earlier. Then, by answering questions that needed a yes or no response, Danny had been able to tell Buzz quite a lot of extra things about the ghost world.

Like: "Can ghosts fly?"

(Answer: No.)

"Can they survive under water?"

(Answer: Yes.)

"Are there any ghost animals?"

(Answer: Yes.)

Some of the questions had been frustrating. Like the last one, when Danny had wanted to add, "Yes, but very, very few." Or when Buzz asked him if he'd been able to find out, as a ghost, whether Mr. McReady, the math teacher, really was a secret alcoholic. The answer had been no—but Danny had been itching to explain that ghosts didn't usually go snooping out of idle curiosity. That it was a terrible drain on their ghost energy if they did.

Danny sighed.

If only they could have carried on a conversation like that, he could have been sure of keeping Buzz awake all night, if necessary.

Maybe Carlos would have better luck, though. Even if Wacko also got drowsy. After all, *they* could talk through the word processor. *They* wouldn't have to rely all the time on this dumb yes/no stuff. *They* could—

Danny froze.

He'd just heard what sounded like a long, low, soft snore.

And—yes!—Buzz's head had sunk onto his chest. His eyes were shut tight.

"Buzz!" he cried, forgetting the other couldn't hear him.

Buzzzz! came the reply.

"Oh, no!" groaned Danny.

For now it was getting more serious than ever. Not only were the snores beginning to rasp out regularly, but—

Slowly, inch by inch, a second ghostly figure was beginning to emerge from Buzz's body. Inch by inch and snore by snore! *An exact replica of the sleeping boy!*

It wasn't the strangeness of the sight that horrified Danny. He'd seen it before, several times.

"It's a kind of temporary ghost," Joe had explained. "The ghost of a living person. It occurs when that person is dreaming a special type of dream—when you dream about yourself sleeping. Nothing happens. Most people don't even remember it as a dream. It's just that you seem to step back and watch yourself as you sleep. It usually occurs when the person slips into a deeper level of sleep."

Fascinating! Danny had thought then.

But not this time.

Just my rotten lousy luck! he thought, this time.

He looked around the room desperately.

Buzz's room was different from either Wacko's or Chester Adams's. There was plenty of stuff in it: books, baseball bats, football gear, transistor radio, small-screen TV and much more. But it was all so tidy. There didn't seem to be a single thing in danger of falling off a shelf with a bang or clatter. Not even—

"Danny! Where are you? . . . Danny GREE-EEN!"

"Oh, no!" Danny groaned, going back to the window.

But—oh, *yes!*

There was Karen, standing in the driveway, staring up. And not only Karen.

"Hey! Carlos! What are *you* doing there?"

Carlos was dancing with impatience at the side of Karen.

"Wacko's phone is out of order, that's what! Maybe the storm. We don't know. He let me out because I'm no use in *there*. We're going to—"

"Carlos! Not *now!*" Karen had given him a shake. "Danny," she said, "tell Buzz to phone right away! It's nearly ten minutes since I left Joe. So hurry. It all depends on *you!*"

Danny almost reeled away from the window.

Buzz was still snoring.

Both Buzzes were still snoring.

If only he could make the guy *hear!*

Then Danny blinked.

"Hey! Why not?" he murmured.

He bent over the bed.

He put his mouth close—not to Buzz's ear—but to the temporary ghost's ear.

"BUZZ!" yelled Danny, at the top of his lungs.

The effect was amazing.

The temporary ghost shrank—withdrew—retracted—disappeared.

The living boy sat bolt upright.

"What—? Where—? Hey! Have I been asleep?"

Danny didn't bother with Buzz's right ear.

He went straight for the top lip.

Buzz brushed it with the back of his hand.

"The signal, right?"

Then Danny touched his right ear.

Buzz had to make the call from the phone in the hall. There was still a light showing under the door of his father's den. But—wide awake now—Buzz was able to dial without attracting any attention inside the house.

Danny crossed his fingers. Would *this* phone be out of order, too? Then he relaxed. Buzz was speaking in a low, urgent voice.

"Hello! Police department? ... Never mind who this is. Just listen. A break-in is now in progress at Hymans' jewelry store, Railroad Street. Got that? Well hurry!

Just in time, Buzz put down the receiver as his father came out into the hall.

"Oh, it's you, son? What's wrong?"

Buzz was so wide awake that he was able to say, without any hesitation: "Nothing, Dad. Just couldn't sleep. Thought I'd get a little fresh air."

Then he opened the front door and began taking deep breaths.

"OK, Danny!" he whispered softly, when his father had turned back into his den. "I guess you'll be itching to see the showdown!"

And he opened the screen just wide enough for a fairly skinny ghost to slip by, into the night air.

18
Shoot-Out

According to Joe's reckoning, it took Roscoe and Kelly about fifteen minutes to break into the store. Kelly was obviously the technical expert. He did all the work on the window and the alarm system, while Roscoe kept watch at the backyard gate.

As soon as Kelly had pulled out the belt of tools from under his shirt, his nervousness seemed to leave him. He worked carefully, slowly and perfectly quietly, using a small pencil flashlight.

Roscoe, on the other hand, began to get jumpier. He kept prowling between the gate and the window— pausing at the gate to peer up and down the alleyway; pausing at the window to peer over Kelly's shoulder.

"Five seconds flat!" he kept saying, in a savage

sneering whisper. "You said you could bust in in five seconds flat!"

"Just a manner of speaking," muttered Kelly, still concentrating on his work.

After that, he simply ignored Roscoe.

This suited Joe perfectly. *He* wasn't getting impatient. He'd estimated that Karen—the fastest runner in the Ghost Squad—could make it to Wacko's house in under ten minutes. So unless she and the others encountered snags, the police would be alerted before the two hoods had gotten inside.

Meanwhile, Kelly quietly chipped and cut and probed while Roscoe fretted and hissed and prowled, until finally, just as Joe was straining his ears, wondering if the police would approach silently or with blaring sirens, Kelly gave the bottom half of the window a gentle upward shove and said: "OK. It's safe now. Watch how you go."

"About time!" growled Roscoe, already sliding through.

Kelly followed him.

Joe followed Kelly.

Both men were now using flashlights. After the darkness of the backyard, it must have seemed like regular floodlighting. Even Joe found it a help.

He was relieved to note that the men were leaving the window wide open, probably as a useful exit route in case they needed to get out fast. It would be equally useful as a way in, when the rest of the Ghost Squad arrived.

Kelly still took the precaution of unlocking the back door, though.

"Come on! Come on!" whispered Roscoe. "Quit pussyfooting around and let's get into the store itself!"

"Not yet," said Kelly. "My guess is that Hyman keeps a lot of the better stuff back here."

The room they were in had a workbench and a safe, as well as a wall lined with shelves at the top and cupboards and drawers below. The shelves were filled with cardboard boxes of various shapes and sizes.

Kelly was more interested in the safe—bending forward and examining it carefully.

"We can't handle *that!*" said Roscoe. "Come on! Let's pick up the loose stuff in the store."

"Just give me a few seconds," said Kelly. He was flashing his spot of light over the safe, from side to side, top to bottom. (Almost as if he were reading it! thought Joe.) "It isn't exactly this year's model," Kelly continued. "In fact, I might be able to get it open fairly soon, if you'll just keep quiet."

"Aw, suit yourself! I'm going in there."

Kelly looked up quickly.

"No! Wait—"

But Roscoe was already at the room's inner door, tugging it open.

And that's when Joe, as well as Kelly, began to get really worried.

In his haste, Roscoe let the door swing open too fast. Its edge caught the corner of the workbench. There was a loud jarring thud.

"For Pete's sake!" hissed Kelly.

"What's it matter?" snarled Roscoe. "They won't hear *that* over in Sharonville. It didn't—"

He suddenly stopped, one hand already moving down his right leg.

A light had clicked on somewhere upstairs. It shone faintly in the passageway, silhouetting Roscoe's crouching figure.

A voice said: "Hey! Anybody down there?"

The men kept quite still. Two dark statues: one of frozen horror, the other of coiled ferocity.

A woman's voice—fainter, shakier—said: "*Was* it anything, Harry?"

A creak of a floorboard came from up above.

"No. Maybe not."

"Well stay up here, Harry, *please!* Please don't go down there!"

"Don't worry, honey. The alarm would have gone off if it had been an intruder. I'm thinking maybe it was something to do with the storm."

Another creak.

Roscoe was beginning to fumble with the bottom of his right leg.

"Harry! The *alarm* might have been affected by the storm! Please don't go down there. I—I'll call the police right away."

That was enough for Roscoe.

"I'm going up there now! We gotta put a stop to *that!*"

"No! Let's—*Roscoe!*"

Roscoe was already on his way.

"Hold it, up there!" he shouted. "Yes, you! This is a

gun. Tell her to put that phone down or I'll blow you away. . . . Ya hear me, lady? I—"

Mr. Hyman must have dived for cover.

There was a shot, a scream, and the bang of a door being closed in a hurry.

Joe ran out into the passageway. Roscoe was pounding up the stairs, two at a time. There was no sign of Mr. Hyman. He must have made it.

But Roscoe seemed to have gone completely mad.

He began to kick the door opposite the top of the stairs.

Joe was standing behind Roscoe now, but he was feeling totally useless. What, what, what—he wondered—had become of Karen and the others?

Roscoe had left off kicking. He pointed his gun at the lock.

"I'm coming in—ya hear?"

"You're staying right there, mister! Police! Drop that gun!"

Detective Grogan and a uniformed officer were at the bottom of the stairs, their guns trained on Roscoe. Behind them, covered by another uniformed cop, Kelly came into view with his hands behind his head.

"Do like they say, Roscoe!" he called out, in a croaky frightened voice.

And behind *him*, anxious and equally scared, came Karen, Carlos and Danny.

Roscoe made a gargling noise. Flecks of froth appeared at the corners of his snarling mouth.

"You go to—"

He didn't finish. He'd started to squeeze the trigger. The guns below barked first.

The two shots both went through Joe on the way to the target.

Joe didn't feel a thing, of course.

But Roscoe did.

With a strange stifled scream, he suddenly crumpled up and slumped to the floor of the landing. Blood began to soak his shirt.

"Call an ambulance!" said Grogan, as he came crashing up the stairs.

19

Detective Grogan Gets Close

The following morning, the Ghost Squad and its two assistants were able to meet early, since it was a Saturday. It also meant they were able to compare notes before Buzz's and Wacko's appointment with Detective Grogan.

"He phoned just after breakfast," said Wacko. "He sounded—well—sort of pleased. But curious."

"*Be careful, though,*" came the caution over the word processor. "*He'll still be dying to know who tipped you off.*"

"Maybe," said Buzz. "But at least he didn't say anything about us being in trouble, when Mrs. Williams asked him. Right, Wacko?"

"No. He said it was just to thank us for being helpful in tracing a stolen trailer. He wants to see us at eleven-thirty."

"OK. But if he should start leaning on you, remember this. He won't want anyone to know how close he came to blowing it."

It was a clear sparkling morning. Detective Grogan was all for enjoying the weather.

"Glad you could make it," he said, greeting them at the front desk. His face looked weary, but the smile was genuine. "Let's go sit by the fountain. It's just an informal chat. Off the record."

He led the way out into the garden space at the front.

"Maybe you'll feel more like talking out here," he said, sitting on a bench at the side of the fountain and motioning them to do the same.

By "you" he meant Buzz and Wacko. He'd have been shocked to realize that four other tongues were already loosening up around him.

"Oh-oh! What did I tell you?" said Joe. "It's what the Police Academy calls the Soft Approach."

"They'll be OK," said Karen. "So long as they keep their heads."

"Wacko's no fool," said Carlos.

"Buzz either," said Danny.

Detective Grogan was staring straight into Buzz's eyes.

"I had them play back a recording of the alarm call," he said quietly. "And I think I recognized the voice."

The only sounds for the next few seconds came from the splashing water and the rumble of traffic in the street.

"Which alarm call are you—?" Buzz began.

Then he shrugged, and grinned. Grogan was smiling again.

"You still won't say who originally tipped you off, will you? But listen—just to satisfy my—uh—ordinary non-professional curiosity—tell me one thing. Was it the same person who tipped you off last night? To tell you the break-in was taking place?"

"Well—uh—"

Buzz looked at Wacko.

Wacko made up his mind.

"Yes, sir. We can tell you that. It was the same—uh—person."

Weary though he must have been, Grogan was quick to pounce.

"There seems to be some doubt about the *nature* of your informant."

The words were for Wacko, but the eyes were still fixed on Buzz.

Buzz felt his cheeks start to flush.

"OK!" said Wacko, stung. "Let's just say I'm psychic!"

Slowly, the detective's eyes turned to Wacko. There was a gleam in them now—as if he'd pressed the right button and knew it.

He nodded.

"I see!" he murmured. Then he turned back to

Buzz. "I seem to remember you had another buddy who was psychic. And you know what happened to *him!*"

"That's right!" Now it was Buzz's turn to feel annoyed. "Danny Green. He—he passed on."

"Oh boy!" murmured Joe Armstrong, "I warned them! I told them this guy would worm it out of them if they weren't careful!"

Detective Grogan was nodding lazily.

"After getting into a dangerous situation, right?"

"Sir?"

"Danny Green *died* after getting into a dangerous situation?"

"Yes, sir. . . ."

Buzz wasn't sounding so defiant now.

The detective seemed pleased.

"Good! I'm glad you get the point. You were lucky this time. But in the future, just leave this kind of work to the police."

"He—he thinks they've been doing it all themselves!" said Karen. "Playing private detectives!"

"*Psychic!*" said Grogan, giving Wacko a gently scornful glance. "You'll be telling me next you made contact with Danny Green himself! Danny's ghost!"

Buzz and Wacko looked at each other. They burst out laughing. They just couldn't help it. Then: "Yeah! Why not, sir?" said Wacko. "Why not a whole *squad* of ghosts? A *ghost squad?*"

Buzz and Wacko broke out laughing again. The fountain seemed to join in.

"But—but you wouldn't believe us if we did tell you that, would you, sir?" said Buzz, after a while.

Grogan grinned back at Buzz.

"Darned right, I wouldn't! Anyway"—he stood up—"I have a ton of paperwork to get through. But just remember. Leave the detective work to the police in the future. . . . *Ghost Squad!*"

He was still chuckling and shaking his head as he walked back to the building.

The two boys and their four companions watched him go—his tall, bulky, very solid figure broken into fragments by the intervening jets and plumes of the fountain, so that for a few seconds he almost looked like a ghost himself.

J
HIL

Hildick, E. W.

The Ghost Squad breaks through